A Fitting End

(A Spicetown Spin-Off)

A Carom Seed Cozy

Sheri Richey

Copyright © 2024 Sheri S. Richey. All rights reserved. No part of this book may be reproduced or transmitted in any form or by any means, electronic or mechanical, including photocopying, recording or by an information storage or retrieval system now known or hereto after invented—except by a reviewer who may quote brief passages in a review to be printed in a magazine or newspaper—without permission in writing from the publisher.

For further information, contact the publisher: Cagelink

The author assumes no responsibility for errors or omissions that are inadvertent or inaccurate. This is a work of fiction and is not intended to reflect actual events or persons.

ISBN: 978-1-64871-500-6

Front Cover art by Mariah Sinclair

Spicetown Mysteries

Welcome to Spicetown

A Bell in the Garden

Spilling the Spice

Blue Collar Bluff

A Tough Nut to Crack

Chicory is Trickery

The No Dill Zone

Cons & Quinces

Silent Night Dynamite

Keslar Mansion Mysteries
(A Spicetown Spin-off)

Cat In Cahoots

Cat Incognito

Cat In Control

Carom Seed Cozy Mysteries
(A Spicetown Spin-off)

Murder All Sewn Up

Tailor Made Terror

A Fitting End

Romance by Sheri Richey:

The Eden Hall Series:
Finding Eden
Saving Eden
Healing Eden
Protecting Eden
Completing Eden
∞
Willow Wood
Knight Events

Chapter 1

Peggy Cochran struggled to get a six-foot aluminum ladder out of the front door of the Carom Seed Craft Corner, banging it against the door frame several times until people on Fennel Street were staring. Arlene Emery jumped up to hold the door open for her.

"Now, just what do you think you're going to do once you get up that ladder? That sign weighs more than you do!" Arlene stood on the sidewalk with both hands parked at her waist and looked up at the large sign displayed over the door of the business next door.

Peggy pulled the ladder apart and secured it before looking up. "I want to see how they attached it. The right side is lower than the left, and it's driving me crazy."

Peggy had recently bought the tiny storefront next

to the Carom Seed Craft Corner and was opening a shipping business there called *The Salty Shipper*. When town benefactors had donated funds to paint the storefronts on Fennel Street, she had chosen royal blue and white before they hung her new wooden sign with a nautical flare.

"And then what? Knowing how it's attached will not make it any easier to fix."

"So, you do see that it needs to be fixed." Peggy pointed a finger at Arlene as she climbed the ladder.

Arlene shook her head and laughed. "I didn't say that!"

"You're not seeing it because you are too close. Cross the street and stand directly in front of it. You'll see it."

Arlene jogged across Fennel Street and waved as Harvey Salzman approached. "Good morning, Saucy. How are you?"

Saucy stopped and looked across the street. "Good, thank you! What are you ladies up to?" Saucy's frown turned into a scowl. "Peggy shouldn't be on that ladder! Is there something I can do to help?"

"No," Arlene rolled her eyes. "She thinks her sign is crooked."

Saucy squinted and extended the tip of his tongue in deep thought. "Well, it looks like the right is a little high."

"Saucy!" Arlene scolded him with a smile. "Would you have noticed anything if I hadn't mentioned it to you?"

"No." Saucy shook his head.

"Wait! That's the opposite of what Peggy thinks. You can't mention of word of this to her."

Saucy nodded. "I'm on my way to the bakery. Can I get you girls anything?"

"No, thank you." Arlene walked between parked cars, but before she could cross the street, Saucy yelled back to her from the bakery door.

"Hey, Arlene. If you stand over here, the right side does look a little low."

"Shhh!" Arlene waved a hand at Saucy to shoo him into the bakery and then glanced across the street to see if Peggy heard. Peggy was climbing down the ladder as Arlene walked back across the street.

"There's a bolt into the brick of the building and then the bolt has a chain attached. The chain attaches to the back of the sign."

"Really?" Arlene raised her eyebrows. "I don't see any chain."

"That's because it only has a couple of links and it's hidden behind the sign. The problem is that the sign has to come down and the bolt on the back of the sign has to be moved down a smidgen."

"Or you could raise the other side." Arlene

shrugged her shoulders up and let them fall. "Or you could just stop looking up."

Peggy laughed. "I guess for today, I'll just have to stop looking up, at least until I can find someone who can fix it. What did Saucy say? I saw you talking to him. Did he think it looked crooked?"

"He said it looked crooked one way when he was on my left and the other way when he was on my right. I guess that makes sense. Unless you are directly across the street, your perspective is off."

"Nobody will be standing directly across the street since that storefront is vacant again." Peggy folded up the ladder and Arlene held the door open for her, although she still banged it against the door frame.

"Maybe Mr. Patterson would adjust your sign."

"I'd rather live with it crooked. I have paid the man, and our business has concluded. I don't want to reach out to him again. He lives in Paxton now, and I doubt he would make the drive over for such a small job."

Peggy had hired Patterson Construction to put a doorway between her craft store and the new shipping store so she could access both from the inside. It should have been a fairly simple job, but she and Mr. Patterson had struggled to communicate effectively with each other.

"What about the painters? Cora Mae might know who they were. If they put it up, they should fix it."

Peggy nodded, still miffed that they hung the sign when she was not around to see it. "I'll ask her and see if she knows. For right now, I'm going to try to ignore it." Peggy shook her head at that bizarre notion. "David and Angela Duffy should be here any minute. She's bringing by an alteration."

"Those alterations have really been picking up for you this summer!" Arlene opened Sully's cage door and motioned for him to walk in. He knew that meant they were getting company, so he strolled in willingly and scratched at his blanket until he got it exactly right.

"It's cheaper to fix something you have, than buy something new."

Arlene nodded. "I'm always mending something."

"Oh, and this afternoon, Volker Electric is coming by to check out the back doors and give me an estimate for cameras."

"Are you really going through with that?" Arlene thought Peggy had forgotten about it, but now she had two back doors and neither had a window.

"I think the package pickups will be at the alley entrance, so I feel like it's even more important now. They are going to put a doorbell back there too, because I want to know who is there before I open it."

"Are you going to be ready for opening day?" Arlene was not yet comfortable with the shipping process, but Peggy knew what she was doing.

"Yes, we're ready!" Peggy punched the air with a confident fist. She was prepared to start seeing income from all the hard work they had been through. "Ed Poindexter is printing a story about our grand opening this weekend, so the whole town will know we're in business."

"How nice of him!" Arlene squealed.

"It wasn't his idea." Peggy raised one eyebrow and smirked. "I had to remind him that he owes me."

Arlene chuckled. "Oh, here comes Angela."

The bells attached to the top of the door jingled and jangled as Angela came in with arms outstretched to hug Peggy and Arlene. David followed behind, carrying a large white box.

"Peggy! Arlene! How great to see you both! The store looks wonderful, and I was so excited to hear you are expanding next door. We really need a local shipper, don't we, David?"

David nodded although Angela didn't wait for his response.

"More room means more product, right, girls? You can spill over into the next room a little, add a few more things. I started playing around with felting this winter. I just taught myself online and I'm not very good, but I enjoy it, all that stabbing." Angela mimicked the action of stabbing a ball of wool with a needle. "It really takes away the stress! Have you ever tried it? Some people can really create realistic animals out of it. It's amazing! You should try it."

Peggy nodded, relieved at reaching a break for momentary silence. Angela was exhaustingly animated.

"I have seen those." Arlene pointed at Angela. "There was a woman who had some for sale at the 4th of July craft fair. The little forest creatures were beautiful."

"See! I'm telling you; you should try it." Angela's eyes darted around the room before pointing at the fabric cutting table. "David, maybe you could put that box over there."

"Let's go to the back." Peggy turned to lead them to the seating area at the rear of the store. "There's a table back here. What do you have there?"

Angela squealed. "Oh, I can't wait to tell you all about it!"

Peggy smiled as she took a seat in the side chair. "I can't wait to hear." David and Angela sat on the sofa as Arlene rushed off to answer the phone.

Angela reached for the box lid and then drew back her hand. "You remember Valerie, our daughter?"

"Sure. She's in vet school."

Angela released another squeal accompanied by a waving fist and a glance at David. "Not anymore! She's home. My Valerie is home, and she's going to start working at the Spicetown Animal Clinic with Hymie Morgan!"

"That's great! I'm glad to hear that. I use Dr. Morgan, so I'm sure I'll see her there. It'll be good to have a second doctor available. I'm sure Hymie will love having some help."

"Well, she's not passed the boards yet, so she's interning to start, but I'm sure she'll do great. She's been planning this career since she was a little girl. Doctor Duffy! Doesn't that just have a wonderful ring to it?" Angela bounced on the couch when her chest rose in a sigh.

David chuckled, delighted in his wife's excitement. "Show her the dress, honey."

Angela pulled the box top off to reveal a weathered and crumpled pile of tulle, slightly yellowed with age. Grabbing the shoulders, she yanked the dress out and stood with it displayed across her body. "What do you think?"

Angela did offer a slight pause, but it was not long enough for Peggy to gather her thoughts, so Angela continued. "I know it's old, but I've already been to the Peppercorn Dry Cleaners, and they think they can get it as white as it was when it was new. So? What do you think?"

"It's, it's lovely, Angela." Peggy stammered, trying to grasp why Angela would bring it to her. Where was Arlene? She was better at this. "Oh, was it your wedding dress?"

"Yes, silly! I wore this almost thirty years ago. Can you believe it? I was so thin back then." Angela pouted in David's direction as if to console him as she placed the gown back in the box.

"Oh, how wonderful!" Arlene gushed, as she hurried over for a look. "Is that your wedding gown?"

"It is!"

"I wish I still had mine. I know I don't need it for anything, but I would love to see it again. I loaned mine to a friend many years ago." Arlene swooned from her memories, and Peggy fought her instinct to roll her eyes. She glanced at David seeking an ally, but saw he was just as engulfed in Angela's memories as Arlene.

"So, what are your plans for the dress?" Peggy raised her eyebrows and stared at Angela. The dress looked like a size eight and Angela did not.

Angela squeezed her hands together and looked up as she took a calming breath, "Valerie is getting married!"

Chapter 2

Peggy sat at a small table just inside the door of the Caraway Cafe, fidgeting with the credit card in her hand, tapping it and turning it against the tabletop, as she waited for her lunch order to be ready. Peggy and Arlene frequently picked up the lunch special from Dorothy and Frank Parish's cafe. but they had ordered from the menu today, which took a little longer. Peggy did not trust herself to eat today's special, chicken and dumplings, on her lap without making a mess. When she saw Frank peek through the pickup window and wave at her, she jumped up from her seat.

"There you go, Peg." Frank pushed two Styrofoam containers across the counter and smiled. "If you see Dot out there, can you tell her I need her in the kitchen when she has a chance?"

"Sure thing, Frank. Thanks." Peggy carried the containers to the cash register and saw Dorothy ringing up a takeout order for Daniel Farrell, Mavis Bell's son.

Standing behind Daniel, Peggy couldn't avoid overhearing that Daniel's credit card was being rejected.

"I'm sorry, hon, but it declined again. Do you have anything else?" Dorothy handed the credit card back to Daniel as he patted his pockets for his wallet.

"Here!" Peggy offered Dorothy her card. "Why don't you just put this all together?"

"Oh, Peggy." Daniel stepped to the side in surprise. "I didn't see you there. Thank you, but I can't let you do that."

"Sure, you can! Here, Dot."

"I've got another card on me. That's my mom's new business account card and I think maybe I've just worn it out. She's had me running all over the country picking up supplies and materials the last few days."

Dorothy laughed. "The last time I talked to Mavis, she was running over in baby chicks!"

Peggy nodded for Dorothy to use her credit card for the lunches. "I want to make my contribution to the new business! And we want to be the first on the list for fresh eggs." Peggy wasn't much of a cook, but Arlene was excited about the eggs.

"You didn't have to do that," Daniel said as Dorothy handed him his two lunch containers. "Thank you, Peggy. I will let my mom know that you are to be first on her list."

"Tell your mom hello for us!"

Daniel agreed and waved as he turned to leave. He had blossomed the last few years, finally conquering some dark emotions he struggled with involving his late stepfather, Howard Bell. Moving back to Spicetown to live with Mavis and help her with her latest adventure had put his past worries to rest and brightened Mavis' life, too.

"Have a good day," Dorothy called out as she waved.

"Hey, Dot, were you or Frank around when the sign for my shipping store was hung up?"

Dorothy frowned. "No, I think it was there when I opened Monday morning and that was the first time I saw it. Why?"

"Well, I had it stored in the city shed because Cora Mae told me I could have it delivered out there. They were in the middle of painting the storefronts when they called me for delivery instructions. Nobody told me when it was being hung, so I wasn't around when it happened."

"You don't like it?"

"No, the sign is fine. I had approved it, but when they hung it up, they didn't get it straight. It's higher on one side and I need to get it adjusted. I just didn't know who to call."

"Oh, I don't know either. Cora Mae might know if the city workers did it. They painted around mine, but I think Vicki said they were taking hers down to paint, so she might know."

"Good idea. I'll ask her, too."

"You could also ask around at the next Merchants' Association meeting!"

Peggy pointed a finger toward Dot in agreement as she backed away from the counter. "Oh, Frank told me to tell you he needs you in the kitchen. See you later!"

Peggy weaved around a customer's unattended child as she crossed her store lobby to stash the lunches in the back room. Arlene was helping a young lady decide on a yarn color, so lunch would have to wait until she was free. She passed the time by giving Sully a quick trip outside and was standing out there holding the leash as the Volker Electric van pulled into the alley.

Cecil Ryman rolled down the driver's side window and called to her. "Hey, Ms. Cochran. Do you have a few minutes to show me your back doors?"

"Sure! You can pull your van over behind the next door and I'll come out that way. I just need a minute to put my dog up."

"No hurry!"

Cecil pulled the van down the alley, and Peggy looked down at Sully. "You need to focus, buddy. We've got to get back inside." As if he understood, Sully was ready and trotting back to the door. Peggy had marveled how adulthood had turned Sully into a couch potato. He was rambunctious as a pup, but slid right into relaxation mode once he grew into his paws. She worried she didn't offer him enough exercise, but he had no interest in toys he had to get up for or chase.

As she led Sully through the door, Arlene was in the back room looking for lunch. Peggy pointed to the containers on the table. "I've got to run next door and let Cecil in. He's here to look at the doors." Swinging the cage door open for Sully, he trotted in and flopped down.

"You've got to eat sometime!"

"I will. I don't think this will take long." Peggy crossed the store and stepped through her new pass-through doorway to greet Cecil at the Salty Shipper's back door. "Come in."

Cecil was looking up above the outside door and at either side as Peggy opened the door. Making a quick note on his tablet first, he followed her inside.

"What do you need to see first?" Peggy looked around, unsure what Cecil needed.

"Well, first tell me what exactly you'd like to be able to do. Do you just want to see the person at the door, or do you want to be able to communicate with them?"

"I definitely think I'd like to be able to talk to them. I might be delayed answering and don't want them to leave. This is where my package pickup will be coming.

The other door won't matter so much."

"My suggestion then would be to have a camera outside with a microphone. Inside, we could put a monitor right here beside the door and you would also have an application for your phone that you could use to view the person and speak to the person."

"That sounds perfect! I don't really think I'll be on this side of the store very often, so that would help keep me from running across both stores to answer the door. I could tell the driver that I was coming, so they would wait."

"Yes," Cecil nodded and made a note on his pad. "Where is the electrical panel here?"

Peggy pointed to the back corner as Cecil made more notes.

"Now, are you interested in an alarm system or recording device on this camera?"

Peggy wrinkled her nose. "I have an alarm system already."

"Where is that? Maybe we could tie these together."

"I have two panels to turn it on. One near each door." Peggy pointed toward the front. "I usually use the one up front."

Cecil tapped his pad. "So, you have two separate security systems? Is this store different from the craft shop?"

"It was when I bought it, but the security people already came out and fixed all of that."

"You have a contract with them?" Cecil raised an eyebrow in thought and then shook his head when Peggy nodded. "We'll need to keep this separate, then."

"Will these doors be together? I mean, will the phone application show both doors?"

"Yes, if you want."

Peggy looked at the door between the two stores for a moment. She had gone decades without a camera at the back door of the craft store, and she had spent so much money already. Did she really need an application on her phone to see the alley?

"If it will save me money, why don't we just do the regular camera and monitor at the back door on the other side? I don't need to talk to them. Really, no one should be showing up back there."

Cecil nodded and made another note. "So just a camera outside, a doorbell, and a monitor by the door?"

"Yes! This side will be used for regular business with the pickups at the back, but the other side is more for just security. I don't even have a peephole over there."

"Let's look at that side now." Cecil pointed, and Peggy turned to lead him into the craft store.

This issue arose when she had a stranger knocking at the back door of the craft store a few months ago. She realized that it wasn't safe to open the door blindly to just anyone back there when she was at the shop alone. Someone could be planning to rob the store or hurt her, so she had to do something. It was so sad that after all these years, it had to come to this.

Cecil checked the electric panel and looked around the doorway while he wrote down details and stepped outside. "This will be no problem at all. I'll call you in a day or two and give you an estimate."

As soon as Peggy locked the back door, she heard Arlene call out to her. "Your lunch is getting cold."

Chapter 3

Dorothy Parish held up her hands to quiet the group before introducing the mayor to the front of the room. Dorothy claimed to be the unofficial president of the Spicetown Merchants' Association because she formed it and they had yet to entertain the idea of a formal election, but she was a natural for the job.

Peggy glanced down at Sully, who was snoring by her feet. She had worried about bringing him to the meeting, but he had not been moved by the activity. A few of the other merchants had noticed him when she walked in, but after a brief hello, he had made himself comfortable as if he felt right at home in the Spicetown Community Center.

Mayor Cora Mae Bingham walked to the front of the group with a note in her hand. Her infectious energy set the tone for the meeting. "Good evening, everyone. I have just a couple of things I wanted to share with all of you."

Studying her slip of paper first, she paused a moment to collect her thoughts. "First, I wanted to give everyone advance notice that Jason Marks will be visiting each of you with a container for donations to put on your checkout counter. It is labeled for contributions to the Spicetown Beautification Fund." The audience began to murmur until there was a low roar spreading across the room.

"Now this SBF group is a not-for-profit entity that has an interest in improving our town. It was created by the individuals that are painting our storefronts for us, and this fund will only be used for items that benefit the aesthetics of our town."

Ted Parish raised his hand in the air as he rose from his seat to interrupt Cora Mae. "How do we know that? We don't even know who these people are! What's with all the secrecy?"

Cora Mae nodded. She understood the frustration. She didn't like secrets either, and in these times, one had to be suspicious, but she trusted Jason's endeavors. "You are not obligated to put these collection jars on display for the public if you don't want to. I just wanted you to know that this group is not connected to city government, but it is directly connected to the people who painted your buildings for free."

Ted returned to his seat and Cora looked around the room for other objectors before continuing. "The jars are not to be opened." Cora shook her scolding schoolteacher finger in everyone's direction. "Not by you or by the public. They are sealed and you should not use them to make change. If the seal is damaged, you need to call Jason Marks immediately and he will repair it. His number is on the bottom of the jars. Jason is the only person that is allowed to pick up the jars."

"So, Jason is part of this SBF group?" Karen Goldman did not stand but held her chin up when she called out to Cora Mae.

"Jason is responsible for coordinating these benefactors and acts as a liaison to the contributors." Cora turned and pointed at Bryan Stotlar, who had raised his hand.

"Thank you, Mayor Bingham. I just have a concern about theft. I'm running around the nursery all day and the jar would be left unattended at times. I can't promise someone won't take it when I'm not looking."

"I understand, and it may not work for everyone. I just wanted to alert you to this in hopes it paves the way for Jason when he comes around to visit each of you. It's up to you what you decide to do. I do believe that this is a nice way to allow our citizens a chance to contribute to the betterment of the town, but I don't want you to feel obligated."

Ted Parish popped up on his feet again. "If these benefactors are rich people, why do they need everyone's money? And if we don't know who they are, how will we know if the money is spent on the town?"

"As I said, Ted, I think it's just a way to include the citizens in the goal of improving our town. I don't think these collections will total a large sum of money, but I have been assured that there will be an accounting of the fund's activity shared with the public." Cora looked around for other comments and then glanced down at her notes.

"That brings me to my second item, somewhat related, ... The painting of the Fennel Street storefronts is nearing completion, but there are two business outlets that have not been addressed—the vacant building on Fennel Street next to the bakery and the old Hart & Grace Tax Service building on Clove Street. Soon those of you on Ginger Street, Tarragon Street, and Paprika Parkway will be contacted to pick colors for your storefronts."

Peggy raised her hand and Cora nodded to her. "Are they going to paint the vacant storefronts?"

"Yes," Cora nodded. "They just held them until the end. Jacob Hart's building is for sale. I'm sure they are hoping for a buyer and wanted to allow them the opportunity to pick the paint color. The building next to the bakery has a potential renter, so they are waiting to see what pans out on that."

Peggy nodded a thank you. It wasn't information

she needed, but she was curious. The building across the street had been rented many times, but the stores never lasted. The other merchants joked that the storefront was jinxed. It would be nice to have someone across the street again, but that would mean her sign needed to be fixed. Her hand shot up in the air again. "One more thing. Do you know who hung my sign up? It might have been the painters, but it was done when I was closed, so I didn't see them."

"I can check on that for you, Peggy." Cora's eyes darted to Jason Marks seated in the back near the door to issue a silent suggestion with her eyes. Jason's curt nod indicated her message was received.

"Now," Cora huffed. "One last thing. This Thanksgiving Day I am planning to announce a community dinner right here in the community center. I know we usually have a craft fair in here on the Friday after and that can continue, but on Thanksgiving Day I'd like to offer the town a place to come together to share a meal."

Cora looked around and waited several seconds as the merchants glanced around the room at each other, but no one spoke. "Participation is voluntary, of course, but there are too many citizens in this town who are spending the holiday alone. I'm sharing this with all of you first because this is an opportunity for you to show your customers how thankful you are for them. It will not be a time for selling, but you will be invited to set up booths for promotional item giveaways or sign-ups for information. Displaying products is fine, just not active selling. I'm hoping to coordinate some activities along with the day as well, and I hope you will all take advantage of the opportunity." Cora looked at Dorothy with wide eyes, surprised no one was challenging this announcement. "That's all I have tonight."

"Thank you, Mayor. The chief has one quick announcement before we close the meeting. Dorothy pointed at Police Chief Conrad Harris, who rose stiffly from his chair next to Cora Mae's.

Turning, he held up his hand to speak from his seat. "Just a heads-up out there, but we have received reports from the county that credit card skimmers are being reported around Paxton." A collective groan sounded from the audience. This had happened a few years ago, too. "Just keep your eyes open and check your machines regularly. We don't want them shifting over our way."

"Thank you, Chief. I think that's a wrap. This meeting is adjourned." Dorothy pointed to the back of the auditorium. "We've got some snacks in the back of the room. Have a good evening, everyone."

Sully's large head lifted slowly when he heard people begin to move about. "Are you ready to go?" Peggy leaned forward and scratched his head. "It's been a long day and I'm ready to go home." She had given him dinner at the store before closing, so he cared little about what happened next. Cora Mae and Conrad approached as Peggy grabbed her purse to leave.

"Peggy," Cora said, pausing at the end of the aisle. "Why did you ask about the sign? Is something wrong with it? I thought you went out to the shed and looked it over after it arrived."

"Oh, I did. There's nothing wrong with the sign, but it is hanging a little high on one side and I'd like to find someone to straighten it."

"Oh, well, I'll get the name for you tomorrow. I can't remember where they came from, but they aren't local. They still have work to do, so I'm sure they can adjust it when they are back in town." Cora turned her attention away as Ted Parish approached her.

Conrad stayed behind, waiting for Cora and trying to avoid the snack table.

"Chief, has anyone in town been hit by this credit card skimmer thing yet?" Peggy shook the leash so Sully would stand up again. He had flopped back down on the floor while they talked.

"Yeah, we've had a couple of reports, but they were from people who had been shopping over in Paxton."

"Do they get their money back?" Peggy walked Sully to the end of the aisle as Conrad backed up out of their way. Peggy had never had a problem with a credit card before, and she used it all the time. She rarely carried much cash anymore and her customers always paid with a debit or credit card.

"If they catch the problem right away and call their card, they usually get it back before too much damage is done. Sometimes it opens the door to other fraud, though, like identify theft. They'll go apply for new cards in your name and you won't even know it."

Peggy felt her stomach tighten in fear. Money was tight and something like that would devastate her business. "I wouldn't know a skimmer if I was looking at one. It makes you want to go back to cash only."

Conrad muttered his consensus as Peggy walked Sully toward the door. "Drive safe."

Chapter 4

"Good morning, Angela. Are you alone today?" Peggy held the door open for Angela to fit the large box through the door in front of her and looked down the street.

"Yes, Valerie is down at the police station filing a report, so David wanted to go with her."

Peggy followed Angela to the sofa at the back of the store. "The police station? What's happened? Is Valerie okay?"

"Someone used her credit card, and she reported it to the bank, but they told her to file a police report. It's such a nuisance!" Angela placed the box on the table and sat down. "It happened to David right before Christmas, and they had to cancel our card to reissue a new one. All of my gift orders were a mess."

"That's awful. I heard that there had been reports recently in Paxton. Was she shopping over there?"

"She went over on Saturday to pick up a bracelet

that the jeweler had fixed for her. That's the only place she went."

"A jeweler?" Peggy hummed. "That's odd."

"Oh, they probably have a thief among their employees and don't even know it." Angela waved her hand dismissively.

"So, are we waiting for them to join us?" Peggy wasn't certain how to proceed without a body to measure.

"I wanted to leave the dress here with you for now. That way Valerie can pop in when it's convenient for her. Her schedule is just all over the place, and I can't do the fitting for her." Angela's voice rose when her eyebrows went up as if she were scolding Valerie from afar.

"That's fine. I can keep it here until she's ready. Do they have a wedding date?"

"No, nothing firm at all. I was hoping for a fall wedding, but I think she'd prefer spring, so that's still up in the air, too. I did talk to her a little about the dress, and aside from the sizing, she thinks she might want a few other changes. Is that going to be possible?"

"That depends on what she's thinking about. Has she tried it on?" Peggy was hoping to get an idea of how close the sizing of the dress would be. A big change would mean a lot of work.

"I know she doesn't like the sleeves. Nowadays, the girls like their arms bare." Angela rolled her eyes. "The sleeves were my very favorite part!"

Peggy picked up the dress and looked at the shoulder seams. She could imagine the dress as it must have looked when it was new, and the lace sculpting the arm with a point over the top of the hands was probably really striking. "It won't be difficult to remove them."

"I'm not sure what she wants with the neckline. She may want that removed, too." Angela placed her hand on her chest. "She doesn't like the things I loved most about the dress."

Peggy studied the neckline. The lace attached to a satin bodice could also be removed without too much work. She knew these differences hurt Angela, but Valerie was right to update the gown to what she wanted. Times change and wedding pictures are timeless, or so she'd heard.

"The neckline can be adjusted. Lace isn't as popular these days as it once was. I think charmeuse, chiffon, and satin are everyone's pick right now. They want gowns that flow softly and it's probably more comfortable."

"Yes, chiffon is what the bridesmaids will wear. The dresses she picked out for them look like evening gowns instead of wedding attire." Angela huffed. "Oh well, I'm just an old fuddy-dud, I know."

Peggy laughed at Angela's pitiful portrayal. "Oh, Angela. She will make it look great. Be happy she wants to wear your gown. Just remember, it's important that she makes it her own, too."

"I know, Peggy. You're right and I'm excited."

"Good." Peggy smiled as Arlene walked in and said hello to Angela. Moving the dress out of the way, she offered everyone coffee as Arlene joined them.

"Where are you having the wedding?" Arlene declined the coffee but opened a bottle of water she had sitting on the table.

"At the church," Angela said. "It will be a small wedding. Valerie has been away from town for so many years she's lost touch with her friends from high school."

"Who is the guy?" Arlene rubbed her palms together. "Do we know him?"

"Probably not. He's from Paxton or at least he lives there now. His name is Derek Fields, but I have to admit I don't know much about him. He doesn't come around the house much. She met him one summer when she was home, and they stayed in touch."

"I don't know the name." Arlene frowned and looked at Peggy. "Do you?"

"No, but have you checked him out?"

Angela laughed. "I haven't hired a P.I., but he seems like a nice boy. He's very cute. I can see why she's hung onto him." Angela giggled bashfully as if she was ashamed to have noticed and then covered her mouth with her hand as the bells on the door jingled.

"There she is!" Arlene jumped up from her chair when David and Valerie walked in, but Valerie did not pay any attention to the three ladies in the back of the store.

Making a beeline for the side storeroom door, Valerie bent over and peered into Sully's cage. "Hi there, handsome! What's your name?"

"Valerie!" Angela turned around on the sofa and waved her daughter over as David joined her on the sofa.

Valerie glanced at her mom as Peggy walked over. "This is Sully, and he usually stays in his little apartment here when we have customers, but I'm sure he'd be happy to join us if you'd like."

"Oh, yes. Please come out. I'd love to meet you, Mr. Sully." The squeaky baby-talk sing-song melody of Valerie's voice had Sully's little stubby tail twitching in delight.

Valerie joined the group of women in the back of the store, sitting cross-legged on the floor with Sully beside her. "So, what do you need from me?"

Peggy chuckled. "Well, when you're ready, I'll need to take some measurements, but first tell me what changes you'd like to see." Valerie was a tall girl, taller than her mother, so Peggy was initially concerned about the length of the dress. Her build was very different, too. Some changes might be a good idea to make the dress fit Valerie's style as well as flatter her assets.

"I love vintage, so I don't want it to lose that feeling, but it's a little fussy for me. I'm not as fancy as mom." Valerie smiled at Angela.

Peggy nodded. That had always been true. Angela was flamboyant in her dress and demeanor. Valerie was quiet and reserved like David. As a little girl, she was much more comfortable in overalls than a dress. "I'm sure we can do all that. Your mom mentioned the sleeves."

"Yeah, I know I want it to be sleeveless and the lace at the neck removed, but the whole thing is going to have to be bigger. How in the world do you do that?" Valerie tossed out her hands as she spoke, and Sully nudged her with his nose to remind her that she was supposed to be petting him.

"How do you feel about a lace-up corset back?" Peggy lifted her eyebrows. Since Valerie was more than an inch or two bigger than the dress, a keyhole back would not be enough. "I can remove the zipper, insert some satin backing, and create loops to crisscross satin ribbon from side to side. That way the dress can always be cinched in to fit you perfectly." Peggy picked up her phone and pulled up a photo she had found online. "Like this."

"Oh, I love that." Valerie handed the phone to her mother. "That's a great idea!"

"Good." Peggy stood up. "Let's get those

measurements."

Valerie gave Sully a kiss on the head before standing up and walking behind the chairs to give Peggy room to move around her.

Arlene sat in the chair Peggy had occupied. "So, Valerie, tell us all about Derek."

Valerie tittered awkwardly. "What do you want to know?"

"Everything!" Arlene waved her hands and chuckled. "Where did you meet? What does he do? Where are you guys going to live?"

"We met last summer when he was working at Slim Pickens. Now he's a retail manager for a company that owns a bunch of different stores in Paxton, so they move him around town a lot depending on where he's needed. We're looking for something between Spicetown and Paxton so we can split the commute time. I'd love to live in Spicetown, but that doesn't seem fair to him. He has late hours sometimes, but I'm sure after I pass my boards, I'll be on call and have long hours, too."

"David has been looking for some land for them." Angela looked at David.

"Yeah, I thought we might put something small up for now and then they can build their own place later." David winked at Valerie.

Peggy knew Angela had not worked consistently over the years, but David had provided the family income from the rock quarry that was steady but limited. "I hear doctors make the big bucks, so you guys can build your mansion later."

Everyone laughed except Valerie. "I think that must be some other kind of doctor you've heard about. There aren't many vets in mansions."

"My girl's never been looking for a mansion," David said. "She just wants to bring home every animal she finds."

Peggy bit her tongue before her sarcasm escaped, but it didn't stop her mind from wondering if that meant Derek was just another stray. She decided to concentrate on measuring and let Arlene handle the small talk from there.

"We are looking forward to meeting him!" Arlene gushed. "Bring him by next time you two are in town."

Chapter 5

Cora Mae had heard Jason talking in the outer office with her assistant, Amanda, and was expecting him to stop by before he reported for work at the Caraway Cafe. "Good morning, Jason. What did you think of the merchants' meeting last night?"

"Very informative. Dorothy had some useful information to share and there was a good turnout."

"Yes, she's always had good attendance." Cora smiled with a mischievous glint in her eye. "I think they come more for the gossip than anything else. These folks live for a scoop on what's going on around town."

Jason laughed.

"I always try to offer them something that no one else knows yet just in case Dorothy doesn't have any hot items. They like feeling they are on the inside track and being trusted with high-profile information."

"I can see that it would make them feel important to the community." Jason had such an earnest acceptance of whatever Cora Mae offered him.

"It is usually something the paper is releasing the next day or the whole town will hear in a couple of days, but just hearing something first gives them status. Do you know what I mean?"

Jason nodded.

"Making people feel good, makes them also feel good about you!" Cora propped her elbow on her desk and pointed a finger at Jason. "That's how you win elections."

Jason smiled. "I'll remember that, but I don't plan to ever run for election."

"I never planned to be mayor, but here I am." Cora fell back in her chair and smiled. "Who knows what will happen in a couple of years?"

"I guess you're right, Mayor. I never thought I'd still be working at the cafe. I took that job when I was in high school as a part-time thing."

"What were your plans back then? Did you have a career goal in mind?" Cora had a career goal in mind for him if he didn't.

"That was the problem. I didn't know what I wanted to do, so I just kept working there. I think the world of Dorothy and Frank. Don't get me wrong. They've become a second family to me, and I know they need my help, but I don't think this is what I want to do for the next thirty years."

"I understand and I know they would, too." Cora Mae tapped her fingers on her desk and waited for Jason to take a seat. "You said you don't plan to run for election. Is the campaigning what bothers you or the job you get once you've won?"

"It's politics in general. It seems..." Jason wrinkled his nose in thought. "It seems fake to me. I don't think I could manage the public image and keep people happy, even though I'd try to do the right thing. You can't please everyone, and I'm not good at manipulating other people."

"You can't please everyone. That's definitely true. But you can show them that you are making decisions using your best judgment and with their interests in mind. Politics is only as shady as the players. You can be a good person and still hold an elected office."

Jason looked unconvinced but didn't want to offend. "I wasn't saying you were fake! Present company excluded, of course."

Cora Mae chuckled. "It's just a stereotype, and I didn't take any offense at all. I do the best job I can do, and I don't make everyone happy, but that's not my goal. I have a vision to improve things and I give it my all. That's not much different from what I see you doing."

"Oh," Jason held up his hand. "There's no comparison. I just tried to think of a way to help."

"Exactly! You wanted to help the local merchants,

and you thought of a way to do that. Then you found the people you needed who could help you implement that plan. You and your idea has potentially saved Spicetown businesses and created a new business."

"I just put people together that I hoped would work something out. I was just a middleman." Jason shook his head, dismissing the importance of the loans he helped Peggy and Ted Parish get through secret backers.

"You're right and that's all I am, too. I have ideas to help the town, and I work with the City Council to see how we can implement them."

"Well," Jason shrugged with partial agreement. "That's on a very different scale."

"Yes, but I had to start somewhere, too. I wish I'd thought of the idea you had. It was brilliant, and you didn't stop at just that. You've accomplished even more with the new fund for town improvements—the new paint and money for the street benches! You're even including the community in the planning and implementing with the donation jars. You are being a mini mayor!" Cora splayed her fingers and held her palms up. "Surely, you can see that."

Jason tossed his head back in laughter to release the tension of the self-examination. "Now, you've given me a brilliant idea! That's what I'll call my master's thesis: My Experience as a Mini-Mayor!"

Cora Mae laughed but then shook her head. She

didn't want Jason to downplay the importance of what he'd accomplished. "So, you can write your paper and go back to the cafe leaving Amanda to manage what you've started, or you can stay with it and look for ways to grow. What do you think?"

"I don't know." Jason's expression darkened as if a stage curtain had fallen across his face. With his eyebrows pinched together, he sighed. "Hmm, I hadn't made any long-range plans."

"You've started something that requires ongoing management because you are the liaison. You are the link between these business owners and their secret benefactors. Amanda has helped you, sure, but they didn't make any deals with Amanda. They made them with you."

"I didn't mean to make more work for Amanda. I guess I need to give this some more thought."

"Well, while you're thinking on that, I could use whatever ideas you have for Thanksgiving, too. How can we organize a potluck for a whole town? I don't want to end up with 200 pumpkin pies and no potatoes!" Cora jumped up from her chair as Jason's somber mood lifted. "We need some way to organize people that want to participate and keep a balanced menu."

Jason smiled as he stood up. "That will be a challenge."

"Not to mention activities!" Cora stabbed her

finger in the air. "Maybe some adult games like bingo, trivia or a cake walk. We can section one corner of the auditorium for the kids, but they'll need someone to manage crafts or games. There are a lot of moving parts to this crazy idea I have, and I don't have all the answers."

Cora Mae smiled when she saw Jason look off to the side of the room as if the wheels in his mind were starting to turn. "The good part is that we have lots of time. Something this big can't be done in a day. You think on it and let me know what you come up with so we can compare notes next week."

"Maybe a winter clothing drive or holiday toy drive could be done at the same time. They could bring those with them if they don't bring a dish. You could do a silent auction with donations from the vendors and that could go into the beautification fund for playground equipment in the park. I don't know if we want to complicate things that much though." Jason chewed his bottom lip.

Cora Mae's heart swelled as she knew she'd found that special person who she could groom to fill her shoes someday, whether he knew it yet or not. "I like the way you think!"

"Just one thing," Jason said as he paused and turned around at the door. "What's a cake walk?"

Amanda was at her desk in the outer office, and she

giggled when she heard Jason's parting comment. "That's exactly what I asked!"

"What is it?" Jason looked at Amanda.

"It's a lost art! You two are too young to understand." Cora Mae scolded.

"I had to google it." Amanda whispered with a smile.

"You don't need the Internet!" Cora Mae huffed. "Just go home and ask your mothers. They'll know!"

"Hey, Conrad!" Ted Parish raised a hand in the air in greeting from behind the pharmacy counter when Chief Harris walked over to the register. "I missed you at coffee this morning."

"Yeah, Ted. Sorry about that. I got caught up on the phone early this morning and didn't make it down to the bakery." Patting his stomach, he chuckled. "Maybe I'll drop a pound today."

"Well, don't waste away on us!" Ted, who didn't have an ounce of fat on him, laughed heartily as he dropped a pill bottle into a small white bag and stuck a label on the front. "What can I get you today?"

"Just a minute of your time. I wanted to take a look

at your credit card machines if you don't mind. You know we've got reports on card skimmers in the area, so I just thought I'd check around with everyone nearby."

"Oh, I'd know if something like that happened. I keep a close eye on those things." Ted shook his head in disgust. "These people should put a little effort into an honest living instead of trying to bamboozle innocent folks."

"I agree, but they've gotten sophisticated. You can't always see them anymore. They've got a device they can plant inside now. It's just a little computer chip, and it steals the number and transmits the information right to the thieves. Do you care if I pop the top off of these and take a peek?"

"Course not! Go ahead and check. I already tugged on the top of them and tested the buttons to see if they felt funny. They seemed okay to me. Nobody reported anything in town, have they?"

"Yes, I had a report this morning, but the young lady had also shopped in Paxton."

"Ah, well there's your problem!"

"Perhaps, but I want to keep a watch just in case." Conrad hesitated to tell Ted that she listed his store as another vendor she had visited within the last few days. Conrad removed the cover from the machine but didn't see anything irregular. "Looks okay. I'll just check the others while I'm here."

"Help yourself, Connie!"

Chapter 6

"There you go, Ms. Cochran. Come take a look."

Peggy put down the embroidery floss she was sorting and walked outside with her hand shading her eyes. It was a bright day, and she was looking up at the sun. "Let me walk across the street. It's too close to see."

Cutting between parked cars, Peggy backed up directly in front of the sign and studied it. Remembering Saucy's observations, she walked left and then right to scrutinize that perspective. Her approval would be the final word, so she had to be certain.

Returning to the sidewalk, she nodded. "It looks okay. Did you put a level on it?" Even she knew to do that much, and she was no carpenter.

"Yes, ma'am." The painter glanced at his partner and gave Peggy a toothy grin.

"How did you adjust it without taking it down?" Peggy looked up, trying to peer behind the sign where the bolts were attached.

"We just adjusted the links a little. It seemed to only be a smidgen off. It probably dropped a bit when we hoisted it up there. I think it's all hunky-dory now if you're happy."

Peggy frowned at the happy painter and his young sidekick, sensing a conspiratorial alliance before shrugging in defeat. She didn't know what secret magic they had worked but her cynicism was clouding her acceptance. "Okay, thanks guys. I appreciate you taking a look at it for me."

"Peggy!" Arlene popped her head out of the front door of The Salty Shipper with a look of urgency. "Cecil is here to see you."

Following Arlene in the front door, she flipped the deadbolt lock behind her. They weren't officially open until tomorrow and the monitor at the back door had been blinking off and on, so she had called Volker Electric.

"Hey, Cecil. I appreciate that you could make it out today. I think we might have a short in this one." Peggy pointed at the monitor.

"I'm going to switch out the monitor first and see if that does it." Cecil squatted down and opened his toolbox. "If it's still blinking, we know it's the wiring."

Peggy glanced out the front window at the painters who were looking up at her sign. As they closed up their ladder, she saw Clyde Newman standing in front of the empty storefront next to the bakery talking with a young woman. Vicki might be getting a new neighbor soon.

"I've got to run out to my van. Be right back." Cecil pushed through the back door and Peggy waited to let him back inside. She watched him struggle to get his arms around a large box and then put it under his arm, so Peggy held the door open for him.

"So, are you all ready for your grand opening tomorrow? I saw the article in the newspaper."

Peggy had been pleased with Ed Poindexter's efforts to give her a prominent headline for the new store. She felt his debt was repaid now, even though it's difficult to compare putting her at risk for bodily harm to free publicity, but earning Ed's favor wasn't an easy road.

"I think I'm ready, but I guess you never know until it happens." Peggy chuckled. "I expect it will be a slow-moving business. I've always known that, but it's something Spicetown doesn't have that we really need."

"Oh, I agree, and I've heard lots of people talking about it. It's exciting to have something new in town. Everyone will want to come take a look."

The comment stunned Peggy momentarily, but then she smiled. "I'll just be through that doorway. If you need me, just holler."

Leaving Cecil to tinker with the wall mount, Peggy looked around the craft store for Arlene and motioned for her to move closer.

"Is everything okay?"

Peggy nodded. "He's switching out the monitor, but he just said something that got me thinking."

"Oh, no!" Arlene teased, backing up away from Peggy as she swung her hand out playfully slapping at the air. "What's next? I don't know if I'm up for another idea of yours."

Peggy shut her eyes to keep a straight face as Arlene cackled at her own joke but ended up laughing with her, anyway. "Seriously, Arlene! Cecil said he thinks everyone is going to come by tomorrow to look around because they'll want to see the place."

Arlene shook her head. "See a shipping place? I don't think I would, not until I had something I needed to mail."

"That's what I thought, too, but Cecil seems to think they'll want to take a look just to be nosy."

"Hmm, I could see some folks doing that, I guess. There's really nothing to see."

"Exactly! That's what I was thinking, but in case Cecil is right, we have to make that empty space look like something before tomorrow morning!"

"Oh, goodness. How are we going to do that?"

Peggy sighed. "We need to move something over there." The Salty Shipper had a large white countertop for checkout and a tall island for people to use if they needed to fill out paperwork. There were scales and holding areas for packages, but there was no decoration other than instructional posters about shipping sizes.

"We don't have anything..." Arlene looked at the stockroom. "There are posters in the back room that the sewing machine companies have sent us. Maybe that would add some color."

Peggy's eyes widened. "Samples! We have all kinds of display samples back there. They might be the wrong season, but they are handmade items. Let's go dig around back there."

After finding a framed cross-stitched sample of a spooky Halloween house, a yarn embroidery landscape of the countryside and a huge macramé owl, they carried their discoveries to the Salty Shipper to begin the hunt for a hammer and nails.

"Whatcha got there?" Cecil had the new monitor up and was switching it on.

"Just some decorations to put up." Peggy paused to watch the monitor and saw it flicker again.

"Uh, it doesn't look like this fixed it." Cecil ran his hand through his hair. "I guess I'll give the store a call and see what they want me to do."

"Okay." Peggy wasn't surprised. Nothing about this had been easy.

"Found it!" Arlene held up the hammer just as the bells on the front door jingled. "I'll get it."

Looking at the blank white wall of the Salty Shipper, she tried to arrange the samples in her mind to decide what was the best plan. Before she could raise the hammer, she heard Cecil tap on the back door and Arlene's voice leading someone over toward her.

"Ricky is on his way over to help me. He's just a few blocks away."

Before Peggy could reply, Arlene appeared in the doorway with Valerie Duffy and a young man that must be Derek. "Valerie stopped in to say hello, so we could meet her fiancé."

Valerie lowered her chin and blushed slightly before waving her hand toward the large tousled-haired boy next to her. "This is Derek."

"Hi, Derek." Peggy smiled. "It's nice to meet you."

Derek pushed through the awkwardness with a boisterous hello and extended his greeting to Cecil, who he seemed to know. He towered over everyone in the doorway and his wiry brown hair looked like a chicken's nest, but it added a few inches to his height.

"I hear you got a grand opening set for tomorrow."

"Yes."

"I really like the way you connected the two businesses like this." Derek reached up and touched the top of the arched doorway. "You can use the same staff for both places! Very smart."

"Thank you." Peggy smiled.

"This is Ms. Cochran," Valerie rushed to finish her introductions. "She owns the stores, and this is Ms. Emery. They are going to make my wedding dress for me."

"That's great." Derek pointed to the back door. "Is Cecil setting up your cameras?"

Cecil looked up. "Just doing a little repair."

"Can I help?" Derek's interest led him toward the back door just as the flickering camera showed Ricky Deavers approaching the door.

"Can I show you something?" Valerie's voice was not much more than a whisper and she angled her head toward the craft store while keeping one eye on her fiancé.

"Sure!" Peggy tossed the macramé owl on the counter and followed Valerie and Arlene into the store.

"I have a picture of a dress I like." Valerie pulled a folded page from the back pocket of her jeans. "It's not the same style as mom's dress and I don't want to change the bottom of her dress, just the top."

Peggy took the photo and studied it. "I knew you wanted the sleeves and the high neckline off. It might be easier for me to take the dress apart at the waist and remake the bodice. You wouldn't need the lacing at the back then because I could make it to your measurements."

Valerie looked to Arlene for advice, but Arlene just

smiled. "Okay."

"What fabric do you want for the top? The picture looks like satin." Sewing satin was slippery work, but it was beautiful.

Valerie's hands fidgeted as her eyes roamed the room. "I don't know one fabric from the other, really. I mean, I know what satin is, but what are the other choices?"

"You could have a brocade bodice. It's a stiffer fabric, and it has a woven design on it. Damask is another similar choice. Of course, there's always lace. I guess it comes down to whether you want it sleek and smooth, or intricate and elegant."

Valerie nodded while staring off into thin air. "Simple. I think I just want it simple. I'd get married in overalls, but mom is set on a church wedding with her dress. It's very poofy for me though. If I keep the bottom stuff for her, I'd just like the top to be smooth and simple."

"What about the back? Open and low cut?"

"Oh, no. Just normal." Valerie shuddered.

Peggy chuckled. "Do you want a train?"

"I don't think so." Valerie's forehead wrinkled. "I'd probably get tangled up and fall down."

Arlene laughed and gave Valerie a side hug. "No, you wouldn't. What about a veil? Does your mom still have hers?"

"I think I'm going to shop for that, and I want a small hair attachment like Amanda had at her wedding. It was so cute! Just a few feathers on a comb with some netting across the face and nothing hanging down the back."

"Yes, it was very pretty. Okay, this helps me a lot. I'll start making a plan. Just don't set a date too quick on me." Peggy squeezed her arm. This could be a really fun project. Having a simple and uncomplicated client meant everything.

"If you decide to have an outdoor wedding, Amanda can probably help with flowers." Arlene rolled her eyes in remembrance. "She and Brian both struggled with that. They did all the decorations themselves and the bouquet, too!"

"My mom is set on it being at our church." Valerie shrugged.

"The church has an outside." Peggy raised her eyebrows.

Valerie hesitated in thought as if wondering whether a wedding on the church grounds could be a possibility but seemed to ask and answer the question herself. She knew her mother the best. It was a shame to see a young girl not get what she wants for her own wedding.

"What do you suppose those boys are doing over there?" Valerie smiled. "I'm sure Derek is probably talking and keeping them from working. We'll get out of your hair. I know you've got a lot to do before tomorrow's grand opening. Mom and Dad said they planned to stop in."

Chapter 7

As soon as the shop door shut, leaving Peggy and Arlene alone again, they returned to the blank white wall. "This might help for tomorrow, but in the long run, don't you think we need to do something with this wall?" Peggy opened the step stool, stepping up to make a mark on the wall with her pencil. "Maybe we should make a nautical theme out of it."

"Oh! Do you remember back when you first started planning this, we talked about selling things over here? I don't remember whose idea it was, but we talked about consignment of handmade items. What do you think about that now?"

"I had forgotten about that. We could keep a percentage for displaying the items and managing the sale. The items would decorate the wall." Peggy nodded. If she was able to sell finished work for her customers, they would need more craft supplies to make more. It seemed like a win for both sides. "I think that's a good idea. We need to make a sign to post here telling people we will take handmade items in on consignment."

"We'll need a contract." Arlene was making an imaginary to-do list in her mind. She always looked at the ceiling when she was trying to organize these things. "I can probably get some ideas online."

"We could mark these items for sale, too. Don't you think? We can always make something new for display."

"We may need shelves." Arlene pointed to the wall on the other side. "Some items will likely be things that can't hang on the wall."

"We could pull a shelving unit from the storage room. We'd just need to rearrange things a little."

"Oh! I just had an idea!" Arlene's eyes widened.

"Oh, no." Peggy groaned in teasing. "I don't know if I'm up for this or not."

Arlene huffed but couldn't keep from smiling. "I can send out an email! We have all those email addresses from our sale announcement sign-ups. I'll send something out telling everyone about the consignment wall. I'll tell them we need their help filling up our wall!"

"That actually sounds like a good idea." Peggy chuckled. Arlene always had great ideas, but she liked to give her a hard time.

"Don't sound so surprised!" Arlene squared her

shoulders and grinned. "Can you handle this? I've got to get online."

"Sure, go ahead." As Arlene turned to get started, they heard the chimes on the door.

"I'll take care of it." Peggy put the owl back on the counter and followed Arlene back to the craft store.

"Cora!"

"Hi, Peggy. Are you ready for tomorrow? Do you need anything?"

"Arlene and I are hanging a few items on the wall. She was just going to send out an email announcement for customers to bring their items in for consignment if they had things they wanted to sell."

"Yes, I'll be right back." Arlene rushed to the storeroom.

"That's a great idea. I can't make a thing myself, but I love buying homemade items."

"I hope it keeps people crafting!"

"I hope so, too." Cora Mae nodded as she walked back and took a seat in one of the armchairs. She had walked downtown today, and her knees were not happy with her. Peggy followed and sat across from her.

"Did Jason come by with a donation jar for you yet?"

"No, but I saw him at the cafe earlier. I could run over there and get one, so we have it tomorrow."

"That's okay." Cora stretched her leg out in front of

her and flexed it. "I just wondered how far he'd gotten. I see your sign has been adjusted."

"Yes, the painters stopped in this morning." Peggy leaned forward and glared at Cora Mae, waiting for her to get to the point. She didn't stop by without a reason.

"That's good." Cora sighed. "I had a visit this morning from Earl Walker."

"Annie's husband?"

"Yes, he came in City Hall to register a complaint."

Peggy sighed. Earl was a quiet guy until he wasn't. He rarely engaged with anyone in town, but when he felt something unjust had occurred, he spoke up. He hadn't been in her store in a long time, so Peggy still wasn't sure why Cora was telling her about it.

"Has Annie been in recently?"

"Last week sometime, I think, but Earl wasn't with her. Arlene waited on her. Why?"

"He's just discovered that someone is using his credit card."

"He thinks it's me?" Peggy jumped to her feet and hollered toward the storeroom. "Arlene?"

"Yeah?" Arlene popped her head around the doorway.

"Do you remember Annie Walker coming by last week? Did she buy anything?"

"She bought some eyes, and I cut her a small piece of lace. She's making a doll for her grand baby. Why?"

Peggy shook her head and sat back down. It was difficult not to take the accusations personally, but she would think the same thing if she were Earl.

Cora glanced up apologetically. "Earl's credit card has some unauthorized charges, and he was concerned that maybe the number was compromised when she used it here."

Arlene tilted her head. "Well, if it was, we wouldn't know it because the company stopped by Monday and changed out our machines after Annie's visit."

"That's right! I ordered a second card machine for the shipping store, and they came to set it up. They decided to switch out the one on this side while they were here because they have a newer model now."

"I could call them if it will help." Arlene worried first about customers and then the store's reputation. "They could check the machine they picked up."

"Yes, if you would." Cora Mae nodded. "That may help put his mind at ease."

"That was over a week ago. He hasn't used it anywhere else?" Peggy used her card almost daily.

"Yes, but they've checked those locations. He went to the doctor in Paxton this week and stopped for lunch afterwards. Both of those places have been checked. He said that's the only time he left town, so he thinks the problem is in Spicetown."

"Exactly what did he think City Hall could do about

it?" Peggy slapped her hands on her thighs. "Did he file a police report?"

"He did." Cora scooted to the edge of her chair. "In Paxton and in Spicetown. I'm worried about the card skimmers, too. I don't want them coming to town, but the chief has been going around checking as many of them as he can. So far, he hasn't found any."

"Well, that's good."

"But Peggy," Cora said as she stood up. "Ed Poindexter is working on a story about this, so I didn't want you to be blindsided if he mentions the craft shop. Ed has a copy of Earl's police report as well as others from here and Paxton."

"Ugh." Peggy dropped her head into the palm of her hand. Just when she had finally found a fair balance with the Spicetown Star. "That's not going to help my grand opening tomorrow."

Cora walked toward the front door. "I'll be here at 9:45 tomorrow morning with my giant scissors!" Cora chuckled, hoping to lighten the mood she had created with her visit. The ribbon cutting was scheduled for ten o'clock and someone from the Spicetown Star would probably be there to take a photo. "Snip! Snip! It's time to make The Salty Shipper official!"

Peggy chuckled. "Thanks, Cora. I'll see you tomorrow."

Arlene waved goodbye to Cora as she walked out of

the storeroom with a printed page in her hand. "Give this a read and let me know what you think."

Peggy looked over the email Arlene had typed up and handed it back. "It looks great! Go ahead and send it. Maybe we'll get some things trickling in next week."

"I found a simple contract I downloaded. I'll email that to Ned Carey and see if he has any legal suggestions for us. We might need to add something to it."

"Thank you. I couldn't do all this without you, Arlene. You are such a big help to me." Peggy knew she didn't say that enough.

"Aww, you're very welcome. This is exciting! I'm happy for you. I know tomorrow is going to be loads of fun. You'll see."

Peggy grumbled a meek approval. She wasn't so sure of that. In her experience, events like this had a lot of snags along the way. She didn't expect this one to be any different.

"I forgot to ask Valerie about her credit card. I wonder if they figured out where her information was compromised."

"And now Annie." Arlene shook her head. "It makes you afraid to use a credit card. I remember the days when everything was cash, but I don't want to go back to that."

"Me either." Peggy shuddered. "But maybe I will for the time being, just to stay on the safe side."

Chapter 8

"Good morning, Chief Harris." Sheriff Lloyd Turner didn't call often, so Conrad was still ill at ease with him, but so far, their interactions had been pleasant. He had only been in office a few months, but he was the first elected sheriff since Bobby Bell was arrested, and the temporary acting sheriffs had all been tedious to work with. Conrad hoped this could be a positive relationship.

"Good morning, Sheriff."

"I won't keep you, but I just wanted to make you aware of some credit card skimming reports we are getting over here. Some of them are Spicetown citizens and others have reported shopping in Spicetown. I've instructed my office to make certain you receive copies of all related reports."

"I appreciate that, Sheriff. I've had a few reports over here and we have forwarded copies to your office as well."

"It seems to be a moving target so far. Every time we think we have a common thread, the machines are clean. We've not had any solid leads."

"The ones we've received so far were from Spicetown citizens reporting shopping in Paxton, but I haven't seen a common retailer yet."

"If it's a moving target, it could move your way."

"We are concerned about that and are keeping our eyes open. If you get any leads over here, we are happy to follow up on them."

"Appreciate it. I'm sending a report over today from a young lady that lives in Spicetown but claims all of her credit card use was done this last weekend in Paxton. The list is extensive, so we haven't checked all the retailers yet, but it's a lot of new locations, many of them in the shopping mall."

"Who is the reporting party?" Conrad grabbed a pen.

"Carmen Maddox. I told her she didn't have to file with you, that we would send you a copy."

Conrad sighed with relief. Carmen was challenging to work with, so he was thankful the sheriff had handled it. "Appreciate it. We'll keep you in the loop on anything we learn."

"Thank you, Chief. Have a good day."

Vicki Garwin glanced at the clock on the Fennel Street Bakery wall and then out the front window of her store. Although it was still twenty minutes before the ribbon cutting, she saw movement through the windows of the Carom Seed Craft Corner, so she washed her hands and tossed her apron at her assistant. "I'm going to run across the street for a little bit. Please keep an eye on things for me."

Vicki had prepared a box of mixed pastries to take over as a grand opening gift. She expected many of her patrons would probably wander outside as soon as they saw the mayor show up, anyway. No one wanted to miss anything and even those that stayed would be glued to the front windows. Rapping on the glass, she caught Arlene's eye, and Arlene unlocked the front door for her.

"Good morning! I brought you a little treat for your send off today!"

"Oh! Thank you, Vicki. Come in. Have you been over to the other side yet?" Arlene placed the pastry box on the register counter and led Vicki to the shipping side where Peggy was still fussing with tiny details.

"Hey there! Have you got everything ready?"

Peggy was a little frazzled trying to second guess

what could possibly go wrong first and welcomed the distraction. "I guess so. Who knows? I thought this would be a quiet day, so I wasn't expecting any attention. With the newspaper article and now Cora doing a ribbon cutting, it's all getting away from me. I'm feeling a little under prepared, but it's my own fault."

"Today will be behind you in a few hours." Vicki waved the worries away with a swipe of her hand. "Don't sweat it. Everyone is thrilled to have a place to take their packages, and that's all that matters."

"I hope so." Peggy sagged her shoulders in defeat.

Arlene waved a cinnamon roll at Peggy. "Vicki brought us treats. You've got time for a roll and some coffee before Cora gets here. Come sit down for a few minutes."

The ladies walked to the back of the craft store to relax. Arlene was right. Peggy had done all she could, and they would be open for business soon. Pinching a glazed donut from the box, she thanked Vicki for the opening gift.

"I don't know if you saw yesterday, but the shop next to mine had a visitor." Vicki wiggled her eyebrows.

"We did. I saw Clyde Newman across the street with a young couple." Peggy took a sip of her cold coffee. "Did you talk to them?"

"No, but Clyde came in for coffee after they left. He said they have a ladies' clothing franchise that they are expanding. They have stores in Indiana, West Virginia, and Ohio already. They start the stores, then hire and train staff. Once it's running okay, they move on to another."

"What's it called?" Arlene brushed the crumbs from her blouse. "Is it something you've heard of before?"

"Sassafras! I looked at one of their stores online and it looks nice. That's why they are looking in Spicetown because they are already named for a spice."

Arlene chuckled. "Any reason is a good one. We've not had a clothing store in ages. That would be wonderful."

"Well, Clyde said they thought the store next to me was a little small, so they are going to think about it. I'm afraid they are looking in Paxton, too. Clyde told them the rent here was much lower, and they had no competition. He sounded hopeful."

"Now if we could just get Jacob Hart's building rented, Fennel Street would be full again. I know that space isn't very big." Peggy jumped at a peck on the window and Arlene rushed over to let Cora Mae in the front door.

"The problem with Jacob's building is that his son wants to sell it. He doesn't want to rent. He was that way with all of Jacob's belongings. He didn't want to keep anything after Jacob died. It's more difficult to sell commercial property right now than rent."

"It's a bigger risk if you're just starting out, but it could be a good investment."

Cora joined Vicki on the sofa and peered into the pastry box, shaking herself as if she was in a quiet internal argument about whether to grab one or not.

"Don't say that out loud!" Vicki shuddered. "Miriam will want to snatch it up. I'm surprised she hasn't already, and we don't need her owning retail property in town."

Cora looked at Peggy. "What property are we talking about?"

"The Hart & Grace Tax Service building on the corner. The son wants to sell it instead of rent it," Vicki said.

Cora Mae nodded. "Jeremiah wants to cut all ties. There has been a recent inquiry at City Hall. There is an accountant thinking about retiring here and setting up a part-time office. He called asking about a business license, but I don't know if he's looked at property yet."

"That would be great!" Arlene placed her palms together under her chin in a hopeful prayer. She had struggled to handle her husband's estate since his passing.

"I think so, too!" Cora slapped her leg. "I hate doing my own taxes!" Everyone joined in the laughter and began to pick up their napkins and cups. It was time to get the show on the road.

"Oh, I forgot to tell you. Donna just found a fraudulent withdrawal on her credit card last night. I told her to go down to the PD this afternoon when she gets off and report it." Donna was Vicki's assistant at the Fennel Street Bakery.

"Do you think it's because of a card skimmer?" Arlene placed her hand over her heart.

"Did she tell you where she'd been shopping lately?" Peggy's concern was growing. Although she did not welcome the idea of switching back to cash, maybe she needed to take her own advice seriously. "What is that now? At least three or four around town so far have had this happen."

"She said she went to the grocery store and by Old Thyme Italian for a pizza to take home to the kids on Thursday. She didn't think she'd used it anywhere else. She said it didn't show a purchase. It showed a cash advance. They got nine hundred dollars out of an ATM!"

"Oh, my!" Cora covered her mouth.

"Where was the ATM?" Peggy scowled. It seemed this kind of thing should lead a trail that law enforcement could follow and nip this problem in the bud. Maybe they weren't taking it seriously because the credit card companies were waiving the charges, but that wasn't okay. A company's loss always came back on the consumer somewhere.

"Out of state. I'd have to ask her again. I can't remember but not anywhere around here."

Rodney Maddox tapped on the front window holding a giant pair of gold scissors and grinned at Cora Mae. "Oh! I guess it's show time!"

Chapter 9

"Good morning!" Cora Mae waved as everyone talked at once. "Good morning! We have a new business to christen this morning. I love the nautical theme, but it makes me feel like I should break a bottle instead of cutting a ribbon!"

The crowd chuckled as a few bakery patrons jogged across the street.

"This new business is not just an additional venture for Peggy Cochran and the Carom Seed Craft Corner, but a vital service to our community. It has been very difficult, especially during the holidays, to manage our shipping needs since the previous provider closed their facility. Peggy saw that hardship and fought to find a way to bring that convenience back to Spicetown. I hope all of you support her in her new project and that it will make life in Spicetown better for everyone!"

Peggy's eyes sparkled with enthusiasm as she greeted familiar faces, exchanging warm smiles and friendly banter. Spicetown was more than just a place of business for her. It was a vibrant community that she was proud to be a part of. The crowd clapped and a few well-wishers hollered words of encouragement to Peggy as Cora Mae wrestled with the giant scissors. With Rodney's help, she finally got them positioned correctly and paused for those that wished to take pictures.

Peggy saw Glen Kirby from the Spicetown Star take several pictures and could only hope they were used for good and not as a way to announce Earl Walker's suspicions that her store had stolen his credit card number.

"Thank you, everyone." Peggy waved as a few in attendance walked back across the street. Those that remained on the sidewalk seemed to be waiting for an invitation. "You're all welcome to come inside and look around if you like. There's not much to see yet, but I'm hoping it is full of items to ship soon!"

Arlene stepped up and opened the door. "Come on in, folks." As people began to wander in and look around, Arlene told them about the consignment wall and then led them all through the opening to the craft store side.

"Thank you, Cora. I didn't expect to have a ribbon cutting for this little place, but I appreciate it."

"Why not? Size doesn't have anything to do with it! I meant what I said. It's a new business and a service this community needs."

Peggy gave Cora a hug, thanking her for her kind words as Rodney walked off carrying the giant scissors under his arm with Cora following behind. Looking through the doorway of The Salty Shipper, Peggy saw Arlene holding everyone's attention as she pointed at the wall to share their plans for homemade gifts and gave a grand tour of the tiniest store in town. She had honestly thought she'd just hang a sign for shipping and carry on with life as usual, but it was evident that would not be the case.

Peggy walked through the store and behind the counter as Arlene led those willing into the Carom Seed Craft Corner where she snagged a few with ideas of upcoming fall crafts as others spilled back out onto the sidewalk.

"I'm so glad you're doing this, Peggy." Joyce Miller leaned against the counter. "And the craft consignment idea is exciting! You've inspired me to go home and finish all of my abandoned projects. I have so many things started that I didn't finish because something else came along that caught my eye. They are taking up half of my closet space!"

Peggy laughed. It was a challenge that all crafters faced, whether they liked to knit, sew, or scrapbook. Everyone had a collection of things to finish or things they'd like to start. "I think it's about time we started our

Tuesday Tea meetings again."

"You're right. Especially now! We need to get a jump on things because we've all got a wall to decorate!" Joyce pointed at the entry wall and studied it closely. "I can already imagine what we can put up there. Mildred has that beautiful cross stitch picture of a walk in the woods. Do you remember that? It has all the woodland creatures in it. She needs to get that framed."

Peggy nodded.

"You may need to add shelves and hooks for all the Christmas ornaments and stockings. I have lots of winter caps and scarves. The possibilities are endless! I can send Bert up here to help hang some shelves for you if you need. As soon as the weather turns cool, he runs out of things to do around the house, anyway." Joyce laughed as Bert appeared in the doorway.

"I thought I heard my name."

"You did, dear. I'm just offering to loan you out if Peggy needs help to hang some shelves. Did you hear Arlene say that they are going to sell homemade crafts here, too?"

"We don't need any more craft stuff." Bert held his hands up.

"Not to buy. I could sell things I've made. I need to finish up those towel toppers and hot pads I started this spring. I can bring them in here and Peggy will display them for sale!"

"Oh!" Bert straightened his shoulders and widened his eyes. "That's got things going in the right direction. Maybe it would even make a little room in the spare bedroom so someone could walk through there!" Bert wiggled his eyebrows at Peggy and chuckled. "As long as you don't run next door and buy more stuff to bring home."

"Well," Joyce tilted her head considering the idea. "I can't promise you anything."

Bert shook his head and laughed at his wife. "Let's go home so you can get started."

Peggy was waving goodbye as Arlene returned to the doorway. "I've got a couple of people looking around over here, but everyone else is gone. I've been thinking...."

Peggy tried not to say it, but a smile curled the corners of her mouth ever so slightly. "Yes?"

"I know it can be dangerous, but I'm wondering how we will know when someone comes in over here. If we are on the craft side or in the back, we might not hear them. We can't have someone sit here all day."

Peggy reached under the counter and pulled out a solid brass Victorian style countertop call bell and placed it beside the cash register. Using a business card holder, she propped a small sign beside it. "Tap Bell For Service."

"Brilliant!" Arlene tapped the bell and smiled.

"This is beautiful."

"It came with the store. When I first bought the Carom Seed, I found it left behind and I used it for many years over there before I put bells on the front door. It's not high-tech, but it's so pretty."

"Much better than high-tech." Arlene frowned. "Speaking of high-tech, did you notice the camera on the back door is out?"

"What?" Peggy spun around and saw the monitor was black. "Ugh! I guess I need to call Volker Electric. I'm beginning to think knocking a window in the door would have been easier. I hope at least the doorbell works." Peggy unlocked the door to reach out and test it but jumped back with a yelp.

"What?" Arlene ran around the counter and saw a young man in a parcel post uniform grinning at both of them.

"Sorry to startle you, ladies. I was just checking in on my route today to make sure I had the right location. I'll be picking up around four o'clock each day. This is the door you wanted me to use. Right?"

"Yes, I'm sorry." Peggy still had a hand placed over her chest. "My camera monitor is out, and I was just opening the door to see if the doorbell worked. I didn't know you were there."

The young man looked up and around the door for the camera.

"I've been having trouble with it since it was installed and I'm going to have them come out to check on it. We just opened today, so I don't have any packages going out yet."

"That's fine. I just wanted to be sure of the location. I won't keep you. Have a good day."

"Thank you." Peggy waved as he trotted back to his truck, then reached around the edge of the door and pushed the doorbell but heard nothing. Closing the back door and locking it, she pulled out her phone, debating on whether to call Volker Electric or someone with a chainsaw, when Arlene returned.

"Arlene, Joyce was just saying that she's ready to start the knitting group back up on Tuesdays again. Have you talked to Grace Keslar at all? I don't know if she has time for it now, but I don't see how I could do it at her house anymore, not with this new business. We could start it up again here at the store though. What do you think?"

"I think that's a wonderful idea! I can send another email out about it, and we could even advertise it in the newspaper. We might get some new members that way. I need to start thinking about doing a regular newsletter. I'm not much of an email person and I forget all about that option, but I know it's all the rage now." Arlene tossed her head from side to side. "As Hobart always said to me, 'You shouldn't leave money on the table.'

That email list is free advertising."

"That's true. We should be asking for email sign-ups when we do events at the community center too, but I always think of it after the event." Peggy chuckled.

"Oh! Do you remember seeing the little turtle and snail display that I made with pipe cleaners and googly eyes that were sitting on the shelf in the corner?" Arlene pointed to the back corner of the craft store. "They were sitting beside the bag of giant pipe cleaners and the children's craft pattern book."

"I didn't see them this morning, but I think they were there yesterday. I didn't move them."

"I hate to say this, but unless they came to life last night and crawled away, we have a small thief amongst us." Arlene giggled.

"It could have been much worse." Peggy hadn't given a lot of thought to shoplifting challenges when she opened this little side business, but it would leave her primary store vulnerable to theft if they didn't make certain someone stayed on that side all the time. What would she do if Arlene wasn't there?

"I suppose I should be flattered." Arlene sighed. "I hope they found a good home."

Chapter 10

Conrad Harris returned a wave from the back of the restaurant when he walked toward the table near the front window of the Caraway Cafe, where the mayor sat strumming her fingers on the table. "I'm not that late, am I?" Chuckling, he pulled the chair away from the table.

"Hm? Oh, no. I was just thinking about Thanksgiving. I may have taken on more than I can handle."

Conrad smiled as he looked at the board showing the specials for the day. "It's not too late, you know. You haven't made any announcements. You don't have to do it."

"I know, but...." Cora Mae shook her head. She didn't have to do anything, but she had a vision. "I haven't decided yet."

When a waitress slid two glasses of water across the table toward them, they placed their order and waved at

Dorothy Parish, who was darting around the dining room like a goldfish in a bowl. She was looking a bit frazzled and taking lunch orders herself, so she was probably short staffed again. Cora felt a little guilty for trying to lead Jason away from the Caraway Cafe kitchen, but she had to keep her thoughts on the greater good. She'd make it up to Dorothy somehow.

"So, did Keith Hanover come by the station today? He was in City Hall this morning and he told me someone had been using his credit card. I told him he needed to file a report with you."

"Yep, he did. Startled me at first." Conrad chuckled. "I thought somebody was dead!"

Cora Mae rolled her eyes. "Funeral directors have normal lives, too, you know."

"Perhaps, but funeral directors are not a normal part of my life." Conrad raised his eyebrows and smirked. Keith Hanover was a special kind of guy, but maybe you had to be that way to find success in his business. Silly, maybe, but Keith's passive demeanor and persistent compassion made Conrad uncomfortable.

Cora Mae shrugged her agreement. "He said he hasn't been to Paxton in weeks. That's what was alarming to me."

"Yeah, he said he's only used his card two places recently. He used it Saturday at Chervil Drugs, but I've already checked out Ted's credit card machines. He also said he went out to Freddie's Auto Parts store south of town last week, but other than that he didn't know what else it could be."

"I suppose it could be unrelated to the other reports you've had. Maybe he bought something online, and the website wasn't safe."

"I'm going out this afternoon to check Freddie's machines just to be sure."

"It can't hurt, I guess. How many does that make now?" Cora Mae lifted her napkin to place it in her lap.

"Five over here, I think. Maybe six. The sheriff didn't say how many they'd had, but it must be a large number."

"Five? I must be missing someone." Cora Mae leaned back when the waitress put their plates on the table.

"Can I get you anything else?" The waitress smiled at Conrad as if she knew he would really like something more. Conrad's diet lately had been more akin to rabbit food, than what a police chief needed. The entire program was making him grouchy.

Cora Mae hesitated, but decided she was not as disciplined as Conrad and needed something more than water to drink. "A glass of sweet tea?"

"You got it!" The young waitress hurried off and almost collided with another waitress coming around the corner.

"I'm surprised there's been nothing in the newspaper about this. Does the Spicetown Star know you've had five reports?"

"Paulie Childers stopped by late yesterday and I told him we'd had four reports this week. I think I had only one or two all last year. Paulie didn't seem all that interested." Conrad sneered. "They never want to meddle when you need them to."

Cora Mae couldn't argue with that, but it did start her wheels turning. "Maybe they need a little nudge. I'll see if I can't find an ear to whisper in over there." Cora thanked the waitress for the tea she delivered and turned back to Conrad. "I'm still missing someone. Did you have another report after Carmen Maddox?"

"Yeah, Donna Wickett, Vicki's assistant. She came by yesterday afternoon."

"Oh! I didn't know about her."

"Yeah, she's another one that says she hasn't used her card outside of town recently. She got groceries last Saturday and picked up pizza for her kids on Tuesday evening. She doesn't remember using her credit card other than that."

"Does she live in Spicetown?" Cora had it in her mind that Donna had a long commute but couldn't remember from what town.

"No, but she's only about ten miles east of here. She said her kids go to school in Spicetown. I think she lives on Pickens Road."

"Oh, yes, out behind Slim Pickens, that little convenience store. I haven't been out there in years! I haven't seen Melvin or Edie Pickens in a long time." Cora Mae dabbed her napkin across her mouth. Melvin Pickens was not a slim man, but perhaps he had been once upon a time. Cora wasn't sure which came first, the nickname or the store name. "They must be getting up in years. I need to stop in next time I'm out that way."

"I saw Slim last year. He had an attempted break-in, and we responded for the county because we were closer. He called us when the store alarm went off, but I think he ran them off himself. They didn't get in, but they did damage the back entry door."

"It's a little deserted out there. That would make him a target. I remember Bing talking about the store having trouble with shoplifting kids years ago. Slim would swing a ball bat at them and run them out of the store!" Cora Mae laughed. "It seemed to work."

"Life's not that simple anymore."

"It sure isn't." Cora Mae shook her head and sighed.

After lunch, Cora walked over to the Carom Seed Craft Corner before returning to city hall. Looking into the storefront window of The Salty Shipper first, no one was inside, but she saw one small brown box sitting behind the counter. Cora hoped that was her first customer.

Walking through the front door of the craft store, Cora waved to Peggy and greeted Arlene, who was at the cash register. Mavis Bell was bent down scratching Sully's head, which made his hind quarters do a jig.

"Hey there, Cora Mae!" Mavis stood up and picked her bag up off the counter as she glanced at the clock on the wall.

"Hi, Mavis! How are those baby chicks doing? Saucy told me you've started a chicken farm!"

Mavis chuckled. "I wouldn't quite call it that, but I do have a few chickens now. They don't stay little very long."

"I told him I thought you were raising plants, not chickens, but he wasn't sure what was going on out there." Cora smiled. "He said he was waiting for an invitation to come check it out. He has chicken stories to tell from his childhood. He was in charge of the coop when he was a boy."

"Oh, I'll have to go hunt him down then!" Mavis smiled. "I don't really know what I'm doing out there so maybe he can give me some pointers. I've been calling Eli Buford when I've got questions, but he's probably tired of hearing from me. So is Doc Morgan! I've bothered him a time or two as well."

"Ah, Hymie won't care, and Saucy will probably enjoy it." Cora Mae nodded. Harvey Salzman loved to help people and it would be good for him to get involved with Mavis' new venture.

"I am actually trying to raise plants. The chickens were just an opportunity I couldn't pass up. I've always wanted some and when Eli offered because he had too many to care for, I jumped on it." Mavis pointed at the clock. "I've got to get going, gals, but Arlene, just make sure your neighbor knows I'm going to take some clippings from your dogwood trees and that fig tree out front. I don't want her to shoot me for trespassing!"

Arlene laughed. "I'll let Margo know that I've given you a pass."

"See you all later!" Mavis slipped out the front door before Sully could stop her, and he walked to the glass door to watch her go.

"Has your pup got a crush?" Cora made a pouting face at Sully when he glanced back at Peggy with big sad eyes.

"Sully and Mavis have a history," Arlene said. "She kept him a few days when he was a homeless pup and he's not forgotten that. She's one of his favorite people."

"Aw, that's sweet." Cora Mae was a dedicated cat person, but she could relate to the love of a furry beast. "So, how is the shipping business going?"

"Mavis brought us a shipment today!" Arlene

waved her hands in excitement as Peggy groaned.

"It was a prepaid return, but at least it's a package. It will give us a chance to test the process out." Peggy motioned for Cora to have a seat. "What brings you down our way?"

"A couple of things, actually. I just finished lunch, so I was close by and decided to drop in instead of call. I wanted to let you know that I got a call about the quilt show booking and they need to reschedule due to a conflict. We can rebook for early October or late February. Do you have a preference?" Cora knew Peggy counted on her events at the community center to supplement her income and the quilt show would draw an audience any time of year.

"I think February would be best. Easter is late next year, and October might crunch our holiday activities. Late February is a nice down time to fill in with some quilting."

"Okay, I'll take care of it." Cora Mae mentally checked an item off her list. "I haven't talked to Eleanor yet, but Amanda said she was contacting me about the next community play. I'm going to suggest a December event, but nothing in the autumn. Two plays in a row seems like so much work for Eleanor, for you, and for all the actors. I think there will be enough going on during the coming months that no one will miss it."

Peggy nodded calmly even though she was jumping

up and down inside. Those community plays were extra work for her with no compensation. She was always glad she contributed once it was over, but during the madness she had moments of doubt.

"I have a tentative booking for a railroad museum exhibit for September. It's something new, but it sounds interesting. It's a mixture of a historical depiction and a hobbyist display. I think it might be something that would involve a few more of the men in our events and relate well to our community since we were originally created by a railway stop for the Spicer Family. I'll have to see if I can build on something from that," Cora said, more to herself than to Peggy and Arlene.

Arlene nodded. "Hobart would have enjoyed it. He was interested in that type of thing." A moment of silence passed, as it always did when Arlene brought up her late husband. Cora Mae knew the instinct to think of those things never left you, but as the years passed Arlene would only think them, rather than say them.

"Sounds like you have a good plan." Peggy glanced around the store for Sully, who had decided to take a nap beside his little crate.

"One last thing," Cora splayed her hand in finality. "I don't know if you remember, but I mentioned something at the merchants' association meeting about Thanksgiving."

Although Arlene had not been at the meeting,

Peggy had told her about it and they both nodded.

"I'm still in the planning stage and I want your feedback. It's a huge project! Do you think it's a good idea, and what suggestions do you have for me? We will need some organization if we entertain a large group of people. Any ideas on what events or activities we could incorporate?"

Peggy shrugged. She felt a little tapped out when it came to free events right now. She had a new business to worry about. This seemed more like something Arlene would embrace, yet even Arlene was quiet.

"Nothing?"

Arlene sighed. "Well, I don't think you need entertainment or projects. I don't know about your house, but my Thanksgivings were just about everyone coming together to eat. The house smelled wonderful, the men would gather and chat, the ladies would fuss over pies, and the kids made their own merriment.

"Too many people are eating every meal of their life alone nowadays. Maybe we all just need to break bread together. I think that's enough." Arlene's eyes were swimming with tears and Cora Mae reached out to give her a hug. Hobart had passed right before Thanksgiving, just before a city election that he would most likely have won. That time of year would never be the same for her.

"I think maybe you're right." Peggy whispered.

Chapter 11

The next morning Peggy followed Sully in the back door and dropped her purse on a chair to turn on the lights. Bringing Sully to work was becoming a job in itself, and she wasn't sure she could keep this up. He was too short to get into the truck on his own, and Dr. Morgan had warned her that he would probably end up being about fifty pounds. She could have planned this better.

Holding the crate door open, she unclipped his leash as he waddled inside to burrow in his blanket. He always wanted a nap after breakfast. As she closed the crate door, she heard someone tapping on the front door. Walking through the craft store, she saw Ted Parish rapping on the window.

"Peggy?"

Flipping on the lights in the storefront, she unlocked the door. It was only a few minutes before opening time, but she didn't usually have customers waiting. "Good morning, Ted! Come in."

"Is the shipping side open? I didn't realize what time it was when I walked down here, and I forget everyone else opens later than I do." Chervil Drugs and the Fennel Street Bakery were the only ones that had early business hours.

"Sure. You can come on over. I just got here, but I open them both at the same time. You have something to send?"

Ted sat a small white bag down on the shipping counter. "I'm sorry, but I didn't even bring a box. Do you have something small we can put this in?"

"I'm sure I can find something." Peggy pulled out a label and placed it on the counter with a pen. "I need the name and address here. You fill that out and I'll see if I can come up with a box for you."

Ted pushed his long white coat back and bent his lanky frame over the counter as Peggy rummaged underneath. She had considered buying boxes, but then decided she would receive enough deliveries in her store to find plenty to reuse.

"This will go out today, right?"

"Yes, this afternoon." Peggy found a flattened box that looked right and taped the bottom flaps to try it.

"Emma Sloan went up to Zanesville to see her sister and forgot to pack her medicine. I told her she could just have her doctor call it in to a pharmacy near her sister, but she said her doctor is gone and the new doctor hasn't arrived yet. The Urgent Care just has nurses out there right now and she didn't think they would help her without a doctor's approval. I promised her I'd get it sent out today."

"That's easy to do. You always keep those things out until the last minute so you can take them before you leave." Peggy dropped the white bag into the box. "Do you have anything else to put in here?"

"No, that's it." Ted handed her the label and flapped the sides of his coat open again to find his wallet. "You opened this store at just the right time! If she'd done this last week, I don't know how I'd have been able to help her out."

"It's nice that you took the time to do it. You know those chain stores in Paxton wouldn't have done something like this for her." Peggy knew Ted had gotten criticism for charging more than the big, franchised pharmacies, but he knew all of his customers and he took care of them.

"Tell Ed Poindexter that!" Ted chuckled, but Peggy hadn't forgotten the ill will the editor of the Spicetown Star had created when he had written a critical newspaper article that recommended citizens move their business away from the local pharmacy.

Instead, Peggy just nodded her understanding of

his angst. "I'll make sure this gets picked up today."

"Thanks!" Ted waved as he walked out the front door. "Have a good day!"

Peggy waved and then looked over her shoulder at the camera by the door. The video was clear, and she could see the alley behind. Cecil had returned yesterday and was working on the doorbell when Mavis' package had been picked up. It had gone smoothly, and she was relieved that all the kinks seemed to be worked out.

"Good morning!" The clanging of the front door announced Arlene even before she called out. "I have scones!"

Peggy walked back over to the craft store as Arlene pushed the door shut with her foot. "I haven't made coffee yet. Ted was here waiting when I arrived, and he brought us our first real shipment."

"Wow! That's great. Well, I got to town early and so I thought I'd stop in the bakery for us. When Vicki stopped me, we started talking, and then I ended up being late instead." Arlene shrugged. "Go figure."

"What's going on with Vicki?" Peggy walked to the storeroom to get some water for the coffeepot.

"I noticed when I went in the bakery that those painters are inside the store next to her, that vacant store, so I asked her about it. She said they started painting in there late yesterday and they are doing the outside next."

"Does that mean someone rented it? Wait. These are the guys that are just supposed to do the storefronts. How did they end up working inside?" Peggy poured a pitcher of water into the back of the drip coffeemaker.

"I know. Vicki said the same thing. The painters come over for coffee in the morning and she asked them about it, but they acted like they just do what they're told. When she asked them who they worked for, they just dodged the question. I think we need to ask Cora Mae about this."

Peggy's eyebrow rose. "Or maybe Jason Marks. You know, Jason is connected to all of this somehow. He has some secret link to these mystery donors. He's the one that hooked me up with this lender and then right after that some unnamed person offers to paint the town." Peggy chuckled. "Literally!"

Arlene laughed.

"He's the one we need to work on!" Peggy looked inside the bakery sack and put her coffee cup down on the table. "The only time I see him is when he's working the grill at the Caraway Cafe, and I can't talk to him then."

"But Cora talks to him! He's working on some school project with her. She told me he stops by her office every few days. She might be able to get something out of him." Arlene handed Peggy a napkin before pulling a scone from the bag for herself. "What about your old newspaper buddy, Ed Poindexter?"

Peggy reeled back in shock. "My old buddy! I wouldn't call him that."

Arlene chuckled. "You know what I mean. I can't believe he's not sticking his nose into this mystery donor story. He can't resist a secret."

"Hm, that's true. I bet he's at least asked a few questions about the free painting going on." Peggy put the napkin in her lap and pulled a scone from the bag. "I don't really have any reason to talk to him anymore. We aren't buddies and I can't just call him up and say, 'Hi, Ed! How are you?' That would be weird."

Arlene moaned when she took a bite of the raspberry scone and tried to catch the crumbs that were falling. "This is so good!"

Peggy pointed out the front window. "Clyde's back over there. He's got a new guy with him."

"I'm so glad the storefront is getting some attention. Do you recognize the guy?" Arlene raised her chin to look over the tops of the parked cars on the street. "He doesn't look familiar to me."

"No, I don't know him either. He's an older guy. The couple that Vicki mentioned were younger." Peggy took a sip of coffee. "I'd like to see it rented, too, but preferably with a business that draws a lot of women in, as long as they aren't competition to me."

Arlene smiled. "You have no competition. You are

far too unique for that!"

Peggy laughed. "Women are more likely to shop here. and if they are shopping over there, they might just stop in here even though they weren't planning to. It will help us get more eyes on our products. I feel like most women come in here with a specific purchase in mind, and I've not done a very good job of capitalizing on that impulse buy urge yet."

"You're right! A ladies' clothing store across the street could really help you. We could beef up our display window to tempt them and find more simple or small items to put around the cash register."

"Maybe if the prices are high, they'll decide to make their own clothing!"

"You don't see that like you used to." Arlene shook her head. "It's not the money saver it once was, and people are always rushing around with no time to do anything the old-fashioned way anymore. I haven't made a dress for myself in years."

Peggy nodded. "I was thinking last night—Do you think we have enough room on the shipping side to set up a quilt frame? It would be nice to have a quilting circle again."

"I think it would be too crowded. If there were people working on the quilt top, someone wanting to come in for shipping would have a hard time getting around them."

Peggy sighed. She had thought the same thing.

"What about the community center? We could ask Cora Mae about using one of the offices upstairs. I don't think they ever have them all booked, and we could leave the quilt frame there."

"But when would the circle meet? We can't be two places at once, especially now with the shipping side."

"Sunday afternoons?" Arlene winced, expecting the moan she heard from Peggy.

"But I need that day off!"

"I know you do, but the only other time would be a weeknight, and I think that's hard on everyone. Those that work are too tired to get out, and the retired ones don't like to drive at night."

"Ugh." Peggy felt pulled in too many directions. "My only other idea was to buy a longarm quilting machine. It doesn't take up as much space. I could put it on the shipping side and charge to finish quilts that customers make. They aren't cheap though and it would take some time to make back the purchase price of the equipment. Do you think there are enough quilt tops in town to make it profitable?"

Arlene grimaced. "Probably not."

"That's what I was afraid you'd say." Peggy shrugged as the shipping side bell rang. "I'll get it."

Chapter 12

Arlene's nose was glued to the front window when Peggy returned. "That was Jerry from the bank. He had a couple of packages to send."

"Huh? Oh, good."

"What are you looking at?" Peggy walked up behind her and saw Clyde holding the door open for the potential renter to walk out and a painter followed him.

"I'm wondering if this guy is the painters' boss. He came outside with the painter, the older one that did your sign, and pointed up at the building front like they were discussing the paint job. Maybe he's here checking up on them."

"Maybe." Sully was finally awake from his morning nap and Peggy opened his cage door. "Do you want to go outside?"

"That's a great idea!" Arlene spun around.

"I was actually talking to Sully."

"I'll take him!" Arlene reached for the leash and

looked down at Sully. "Do you want to take a walk down Fennel Street, buddy?"

"Are you using my dog to spy?" Peggy chuckled.

"I know Clyde. He goes to my church and I'm not spying! I'm being friendly."

"You're going to be the Fennel Street Welcome Wagon, right?" Peggy nodded.

"Right!" Arlene stabbed her finger in the air and turned toward the door with Sully waddling behind her. "Come along, Mr. Cochran, and try not to drool on the newcomer."

Peggy laughed as the two left the store on their reconnaissance mission. Sully had begun to slobber lately, and it was not very becoming, but Dr. Morgan had warned her about that at Sully's last vet visit.

Hymie said English Bulldogs were a very popular breed, although she'd never known anyone who had owned one, but he had mentioned that she shouldn't be alarmed by excessive salivation. She was thankful for the warning, but it was not her favorite part of dog ownership. Hymie had also told her that the folds of skin around Sully's face should be cleaned daily and that was not Sully's favorite part of the day. Peggy told him every night when he tried to hide from her as soon as he saw the wet cloth in her hand that all relationships required compromise. This was theirs.

Amanda Stotlar walked through Mayor Bingham's office door with a long white banner that was actually many pages taped together strategically to show an enlarged diagram of the Spicetown Community Center auditorium. Placing it on the conference table in Cora's office, she returned to her office to grab a box of smaller items she had made to scale.

"What have you got here?" Cora walked over to the conference table and smiled. "This is so nice! I do so much better working with a tangible vision. My head is too cluttered for one more thing in it!"

Amanda smiled. She had noticed Cora scratching out tiny diagrams of the auditorium on her desk notepad as she wrestled with mental images of a Spicetown Thanksgiving celebration. When Cora had a vision of a new adventure, her mind could not be quieted from the planning of it, and those thoughts were disturbing her regular work. Amanda had hoped this large picture would relieve some of Cora's frustrations.

"These little rectangles," Amanda said holding up a blue card. "These are banquet tables plus six feet on each of the four sides. You can actually put these next to each other and know you have enough sitting space built in.

They are the same scale as the diagram here, so that way you can figure out where you want to put the tables and how many you can get in there."

"This is wonderful!" Cora took a deep breath. "It's just what I needed. I guess Jason wasn't able to get away this morning, but we were just talking about this. He had asked me about the dimensions of the area."

"The legend is over on the bottom left side, but everything is made to scale."

"Even if I don't decide to have this Thanksgiving meal, this diagram will come in handy for every event. I should have thought of this myself!" Cora placed a row of blue cards across the center of the auditorium to see how many would fit. It was something she had been thinking about all week.

"You aren't sure you want to do this?"

"I'm concerned about managing the food properly. I could end up with too much food or too little. I won't know what anyone is bringing, and I won't have any way to balance out the menu quickly if I don't have what I need. It's just a free-for-all and I can't figure out how to maintain order of it."

"You won't have control." Amanda knew Cora found comfort in orderly controlled situations. She planned things out thoroughly and didn't like surprises.

Cora smirked. "I like my description better, but I don't want it to fail. I want it to go well and become a town tradition. If I can't do it right; I don't think I should do it at all."

Amanda nodded. She felt any event got better with practice but knew Cora didn't want her name on something subpar. "I think if you get commitments on the meat, the rest will work out on its own. I know Bert Miller has a smoker, and he'd probably love to smoke some meat for the event. Maybe you can get donations from the merchants' association members or rotary club to buy the meat. Bert might even be willing to bring his smoker downtown and cook it at the center."

"But how much meat do we need? Do you see my problem? I don't know whether I'll have twenty people or two hundred!"

"You could sell tickets for one dollar and use that money for turkeys." Amanda's eyebrows rose with uncertainty. "That would also give you a possible head count."

Jason Marks knocked lightly on the doorframe and smiled. "Good morning! Sorry I'm late. Are we talking turkeys?"

Amanda chuckled. "Yes, we are."

"See what Amanda made!" Cora waved at the conference table. "This is such a load off of my feeble mind. I've been picturing this over and over. At least now we can be certain of how many we can seat."

"This is great! Are you going to put a line of tables

down the side for everyone to fill their plate? Then maybe you could put the desserts off in a separate corner by the stage so they could go there after they eat."

Amanda slipped out of the room when the phone in her office began ringing.

"I thought a line of tables against the stage would put the desserts in a nice central place." Cora pointed to the stage on the banner and Jason nodded.

"Sorry I was late today. My neighbor came over this morning to see if Mom was home. He said his bank account had been hacked, and he was pretty upset. I took him up to the station so Mom could take his report and then I went to the bank with him."

"Are you talking about Otis Kittering?" Cora's hand covered her heart. Otis had been in charge of maintenance when she was a new teacher and although he hired and supervised all the school district's cleaning staff, you could find him many days in the janitor closet of Peppermint Elementary School pitching in with the day's clean-up. He kept an office there at the elementary school and the kids all called him Mr. Kit.

"Yeah, Mr. Kit doesn't get around too well anymore and he says he doesn't shop online, so I can't imagine how this happened to him. He's pretty devastated."

"He must be in his eighties now." Cora looked around her office as if searching for a remedy. "What did the bank say?"

"They said it was his debit card. He still has the card, but someone got the number and PIN somehow, so they withdrew all of his money. Jerry said there were three different withdrawals."

"Well, why didn't the bank call him?" Cora threw her hands up in the air. The bank should have known this was fraud and questioned it. Jerry Finch knew everyone in town.

"I think it happened really fast. He didn't have a lot of money, and it was gone before they realized it." Jason shook his head in defeat. "I don't know what he's going to do now. The debit card isn't like a credit card. They don't just let you report fraud and fill your bank account back up with money. The loss is on you and the money is just gone."

Cora Mae pulled a chair out at the conference table and sat down. "Otis probably didn't realize that. I think everyone's stopped using debit cards nowadays, but he may not have a credit card."

"His granddaughter said he has one credit card, but he only uses it for medical emergencies that he can't pay for all at once. I called her from the station and let her know what had happened."

"Emily?" Cora frowned. Emily was a little girl in her memory, but she would be in her thirties now.

"Yeah, Emily Trammel. She lives over in Paxton now, but she comes over to check on Mr. Kit every few weeks. I think she writes his checks for him to pay bills. He has arthritis in his hands, and he has trouble writing." Jason held his hand out absentmindedly and rubbed his left thumb across the back of his right hand as he'd seen Mr. Kit do a hundred times.

Cora cocked her head to the side. "So, when does he use the debit card?"

"Just for gas and groceries here in town. Emily said she has taken him to the store a few times and he uses the debit card, but I know he goes out on his own sometimes. He's still driving, and he told me he goes to Chervil Drugs once a month. I don't think he drives out of town though."

"I'm going to talk to the chief about this. This has got to stop!" Cora closed her fist on the table. "We need to get his money back."

Jason shrugged. "I don't know how to do that."

"That's why we have a police chief!" Cora pushed against the conference table to bolt from her chair and walked to her office door. Amanda looked up from her desk when Cora appeared. "Amanda, will you please give the chief a call and tell him I need to speak with him? Lunch will be fine, but if he's not free then, see if he has time for me this afternoon."

Amanda nodded and Cora Mae turned back to Jason.

"So, let's talk turkey now!"

Chapter 13

Peggy turned around when she heard the door open and watched Arlene wrangle Sully inside with a perturbed expression. Peggy couldn't tell whether it was due to a failed mission or Sully's reluctance to return. "How did it go?"

Removing his leash, Arlene let Sully rush over to greet Peggy as if he'd be away for months, and she squatted down to rub his ears. "Well, I met the man." Arlene huffed.

"Is he a potential renter?"

Arlene huffed. "I don't think so. He seemed to have nothing to share but criticism of the building. Clyde said they were going over to Jacob Hart's building next."

"So, he is looking for commercial property, right?"

"He is." Arlene nodded. "But he's not sure Spicetown has the elite atmosphere that he's looking for." Arlene tried her best to deliver that last line as a pretentious snob, but she was no actress.

"Did he actually say that?" Peggy's eyebrows rose.

"No, but everything he did say was laced with that attitude. He thinks he's too good for us. He gets that point across without saying it."

"I can see you weren't fond of the man." Peggy chuckled. "Who is he and what's his business?"

"I'm guessing he is the accountant that Cora Mae mentioned. He said he was a retired CPA that was looking for a small lucrative spot to offer sporadic part-time services in his leisure years." Arlene tossed her head back. "And yes, he actually said that!"

"With that attitude, he's bound to get the least amount of work possible!"

Arlene nodded and then frowned. "He is really handsome, though."

Peggy laughed at Arlene's scowl. It always distressed Arlene when pretty people had ugly personalities. She struggled with that internal conflict.

"Well, that will only fool the shallow." Peggy opened Sully's crate door and he happily curled up in his dog bed for a post walk nap.

"Such a shame," Arlene muttered. "I saw Chief Harris while I was out. He said he was coming by this morning to check our credit card machine again. He wants to show us how to do it ourselves so we can keep an eye on it. He's still getting reports around town of people's cards getting used."

"When Mavis was here earlier, she thanked me for buying her lunch and I asked her about the credit card problem Daniel had at the Caraway Cafe. It was supposed to be a new credit account that she opened for her business expenses. She had to call the company, but she found out that there were fraudulent charges on the card that hit the credit limit, so that's why it was declined. It was only a few thousand because she had a really low limit, but she had to cancel it."

"Did she file a police report?"

"She did, but she filed it with the county sheriff's office." Peggy made a mental note to add Mavis to her list. She was trying to keep track of all the skimmer reports.

"That's not a good way to start a business."

"I keep thinking we wouldn't be a target for a skimmer. We don't have enough business to be interesting, plus our machines are brand new. The agent said this new model was tamper proof."

"I don't think anyone is safe anymore." Arlene put her purse away and looked at the shelves on the wall. "We have a couple of hours before lunch. I think I'll get those candle making kits priced and put on the shelf."

"Okay, I'm going in the back to pay a few bills. Holler if you need me."

"What's the emergency?" Conrad leaned over the table in the Caraway Cafe and spoke in a hushed tone.

Cora let her closed fist tap the table before answering. "Mr. Kit!"

"Oh, you heard about that already, huh?" Conrad scratched his chin. He was going to tell her when he saw her, but he should have known the news would be out too quick for that.

"Yes, and this it a bit different from the other people that have had their credit cards tampered with. This man has lost everything, and the only way to help him is to catch these people."

Conrad nodded. The likelihood of returning Otis Kittering's funds to him was almost zero, even if they could identify the thief. "You know the money is probably already spent."

"I can't believe the bank won't help him." Cora quivered in frustration and disappointment. "I'm sure Otis didn't know that he had no protection from the bank. People always hear about FDIC ensuring your money and they think that covers theft."

"Most people have stopped using those debit cards nowadays. I cut mine up years ago. They aren't worth the risk."

"His granddaughter said he only used it a couple of places here in town. She helped him pay his bills by check. He doesn't even buy things online."

Conrad nodded. He had read the report and had seen this happen before.

"What are you going to do to catch this person?" Cora glared at Conrad and swiveled in her chair when Conrad waved at someone coming in the door.

Peggy had stopped in to pick up a lunch order and she waved at them both.

"I understand your frustration, Cora," Conrad whispered. "And I'm doing all I can."

"I know."

"Hello there! How are you?" Peggy approached their table looking from one to the other and sensing some tension. "Am I interrupting?"

"Oh, no, dear. How are you today?" Cora patted the seat beside her.

"Pretty good. Arlene was just mentioning you earlier today. She was walking Sully down the street and met a man who was with Clyde Newman. They were looking at the shop space next to Vicki's bakery. She said he was probably the accountant that you mentioned."

"Ah, yes! Did she get a name?"

"If she did, she didn't mention it, but she said he was a CPA, so we thought that might be the man who contacted City Hall. She said he didn't seem interested in that property though. They were going down to Jacob Hart's place to look at it next."

"I hope he finds what he's looking for here. We could use an accountant in town."

"Did you know that the painters who have been doing the storefronts are now inside the empty shop next to Vicki? They are painting the inside walls. Do you know who owns that storefront?" Peggy heard Frank call her name from the order window and she turned to let him know she was coming.

"I haven't been down that way today. I guess they are picking up some extra work while they are in town. Were you looking for someone to do some painting for you?"

Peggy stepped aside when a waitress approached the table. Cora was not making eye contact with her and either didn't want to talk in front of Conrad or didn't want to answer her question. "My order is up. You two have a good day!"

Peggy picked up her two lunches and hurried out the door as Conrad and Cora placed their lunch order.

"Is there some reason you didn't want to answer Peggy's question?" Conrad squinted his eyes in judgment. He could always tell when Cora was avoiding a situation.

"No. What question? I didn't know the painters

were working inside. I haven't been to the bakery since the ribbon cutting." Cora busied herself with her napkin and utensils while avoiding Conrad's gaze.

"Who owns that building?" The tables had turned, and Conrad glared at Cora. He knew it was public record and she wouldn't be keeping a secret from him without reason.

"I really couldn't say." Cora stirred her tea and put a napkin under her glass.

"Couldn't or won't?"

Cora looked at Conrad wishing he would withdraw the question, but anytime he thought she was holding back a secret from him, his questioning became relentless. "I'm not sure. I think it's some blind trust or something. I can't remember, but it's changed hands several times." Cora waved her hand to dismiss the topic.

"Recently? Within the last year?" Conrad leaned forward on his elbows.

"I believe so. I don't recall when exactly."

"Why are you being secretive about this? Did you buy it?"

Cora Mae forced a chuckle and shook her head. "Heavens, no. What would I do with a building on Fennel Street?"

"I don't know, but I also don't know why you won't share what you do know. Frankly, it's not like you. What did I do to be deemed untrustworthy all of a sudden?"

Cora opened her mouth to protest, but Conrad held his hand up with his palm facing out.

"Nope, that's fine. You don't want to tell me; I don't need to know. I'm just head of the police department in this town. There's no reason why I should know if someone new is buying commercial property. I'll just call you if someone breaks into that building or it catches on fire. You can call your secret friend and let them know what's happening. I'll be sure and tell you what's going on since you hold the keys to the secrets of the town."

"Oh, for heaven's sake, Connie!" Cora winced and looked up at the ceiling. "I was telling you the truth. I don't know for certain. I don't want to add to the town gossip by sharing my speculations, but that's all it is. I'd just be guessing."

"I can play that game, too." Conrad nodded. "And I can keep your speculation quiet. Who do you think is behind that trust?"

"Here you go!" Dorothy Parish slid two plates on the table in front of them. "A tuna salad on toast for Cora Mae and a salad for the chief. Can I get you a refill?"

Chapter 14

Arlene sat cross-legged on the floor tucking extra patterns into storage boxes kept hidden below the shelving. "What time is it? Did that pickup guy already come by?"

Peggy jumped up from her sewing machine where she was piecing some quilt squares and looked at the clock on the wall. "Oh my gosh, it's almost five o'clock!" Running across the store and into the shipping store, she looked at the back door. "That stupid monitor is out again!"

"What?" Arlene struggled to get her legs under her and came around the corner of the pass-through door. "What is wrong with that thing? It was fine this morning."

"I've got to call the company and see if the driver will come back. We must have missed him. He said he would be by at four o'clock every day. I can't believe I forgot all about it."

"It's new. We don't have a routine yet. I'm sure he's still on his route somewhere. Maybe we can run the packages to wherever he is. I could jump in the car and find him."

"Wait. Let me call them real quick." Peggy held her finger in the air while she waited for the ringing phone to be answered. "They aren't answering."

"They aren't answering! How can they just not answer their phone?"

Peggy disconnected the call and called right back.

"Are you calling customer service?" Arlene's finger flicked over her phone screen as she searched for an alternate number.

"No. I'm calling the local warehouse. This is the card the guy gave me. It should be the main office in Paxton."

"I could try customer service. Maybe they could tell us what to do."

Peggy nodded. "Go ahead. I'm going to keep dialing this number and hope someone answers, but the office staff may leave at five o'clock."

Pacing around the store, they each waited for someone to help them until Arlene finally got a person on the line. "Oh! Hello, we are a local pickup site in Spicetown, Ohio, and our driver didn't come today. We have packages that need to go out. Can you get in touch with our driver or tell us what we can do?"

Peggy gave up on her call and sat down behind the counter to listen to Arlene.

"Do you have another local warehouse phone number? We have one but no one will answer the phone there."

Peggy handed her the card to read them the number.

"Okay. Thank you." Arlene huffed as she hung up the phone. "She said we can either wait until tomorrow's pickup or drive it to the Paxton warehouse ourselves."

Peggy looked out the front windows and back at the camera. She had promised Ted that the medicine would go out today. She and Sully would have to take a drive, but this could not become a habit. "I guess I'm driving to Paxton."

"Let's just close early and I'll go with you." Arlene didn't know what a warehouse was like, but it didn't sound like a place Peggy belonged alone, and then there was Sully. She couldn't take him home with her, but at least she could help manage him.

"Okay, let's go. We've got to hurry. I think the drop off there closes at six o'clock."

Arlene turned the open signs to closed, locked things up and turned off the lights as Peggy wrestled Sully into her truck. Arlene hopped in with three packages in her lap and got a big sloppy kiss from Sully.

"I'm sorry about that, but we don't have a lot of space in here."

"I wasn't thinking." Arlene shook her head. "I could have driven. My car is just down the street."

"That's fine. I just want to apologize ahead of time because Sully will probably slobber on you."

Arlene laughed as Peggy backed into the alley. "Well, I am in his seat. I guess that gives him the right." Placing the packages around her feet, she pulled Sully onto her lap so he could look out of the window. "What are you going to do to Cecil tomorrow?"

"Strangle him!" Peggy growled. "I can't understand why that monitor keeps going out. It works fine on the other door."

"That's because you don't need it there." Arlene rolled her eyes smugly. "The easiest thing might be to move the delivery guy to the craft store back door."

"Then we have to carry all the packages from one side to another. We will have to make some new arrangements tomorrow for sure! Have you ever seen this place before? I don't really know where I'm going." Peggy drove down Fennel Street heading east to Paxton. She knew the location was somewhere off the main highway near the Paxton city limits, but she'd never driven back there.

"No idea." Arlene shook her head. "I thought it was just where the delivery trucks went. I didn't know it was okay to go directly to the warehouse. I'll get directions on my phone, so we don't miss the road."

"Good idea."

"My phone says it's only fifteen miles away. That's not too bad." Arlene looked over at Peggy as she scowled at the road in front of her probably plotting what she would say to Volker Electric in the morning. She needed a distraction. "Have you started on Valerie's wedding dress yet?"

"I've started taking some of it apart. With no wedding date set, I'm not sure I want to invest too much time there yet."

"Do you think it might not happen?" Arlene stroked the top of Sully's head as he looked out the side window watching the fields pass by.

"Anything can happen, but I was just thinking she might change her mind about what she wants. She may be flipping through wedding magazines and see something different that catches her eye, or her mother may wear her down to convince her to keep the more traditional style. Either way, I know I have to add material to it, so I have taken the sleeves off and started removing the bodice."

"How are you going to add to the waist?" Arlene had watched Peggy work miracles with alterations, but Valerie was significantly larger than the dress.

"I thought I'd add a whole new section on the back

and cover it with a short train that attaches at the waist. It would make it easier to sit down in because she could pull the train to the side."

Arlene's eyes widened. "That's a great idea!"

"I think I'll have to make the whole bodice new, maybe in satin, to give her what she wants. I'm waiting on that part until she's sure about what she wants."

"I'm so excited for her! They make a really cute couple, and I'm so glad she's come home to stay. So many young people go off to college and then move on to new places. It would break her parents' hearts if she did that. They have always doted on her so."

Arlene shrieked when Sully's drool hit the door handle of the car and she searched her purse for a tissue.

"What? Did I pass it?" Peggy glanced over at Arlene.

"No. Sully just slobbered on the door handle."

Peggy chuckled. "I know it's awful, but I'm getting used to it. I need to put a bib on him!"

Arlene laughed. "Did you talk to Hymie about this drooling?"

"I did and he didn't have a remedy. It gets worse when he gets hot. Point the air conditioner vent at him. Maybe that will help."

Arlene looked down at her phone. "The turnoff is getting close."

Once they found the road, the warehouse entry was

hidden behind a row of pine trees and not far from the main highway. Arlene stayed in the truck with Sully and Peggy ran in to drop off the packages. Sully panted nervously when he watched Peggy run up to the front door and go inside the warehouse. Arlene prepared herself for more drool.

Peggy sighed when she hopped back into the truck. "That wasn't so bad. There was someone inside at a counter and they took the packages without any hesitation. I'm relieved. I was worried they would give me a problem about dropping them off and I promised Ted his package would go today."

"I know. I'm glad that's all taken care of. Do you need anything in Paxton? We are so close, and I can watch Sully if you need to run in somewhere."

"No." Peggy shook her head. "I can't think of anything. It's a shame we can't go have dinner somewhere." Looking at Sully, she rolled her eyes. "But you know who would ruin that."

Arlene laughed. "I'm sure he's hungry, too."

"Always!" Peggy backed away from the warehouse and returned to the highway. "I need to get some gas. I'm going to make a quick stop on the way back." Peggy crossed the highway to return to Spicetown and veered into the gas station on the right.

"I could run in and use the restroom. Do you want anything?"

"No, I'm fine." Peggy pulled up to the gas pump.

"Will Sully be okay in the cab?"

"Oh, yeah. He'll be fine." Peggy put her arms around Sully as Arlene opened the truck door to slip out. "I've got him." Once the door was shut, Peggy pointed at Sully. "Sit tight." They had overcome these challenges already. As soon as Peggy left the truck to get her gas, Sully's front paws jumped up on the armrest so he could watch her every move. He still had some abandonment issues, and he didn't like it if she walked away. When she had needed to go inside to pay, she'd tucked him under her arm and taken him with her. He was getting a little big for that now.

When Arlene returned, Peggy was already back in the truck waiting for her and Sully was dancing around excited to see her approaching. "I'm back!" Arlene quickly shut the door and then reached for Sully, dismayed to see that the joyfulness also seemed to make him drool. "You'll never believe who I saw inside!"

"Who?" Peggy pulled the truck back out onto the highway.

"Valerie Duffy and her husband-to-be!"

Chapter 15

Officer Gwen Kimball peeked in Conrad's open office door. "Good morning. Did you need to see me, Chief?"

"Yeah, Kimball. Have a seat." Conrad waved her to the chair opposite his desk and shuffled the folders in front of him. The paperwork had been multiplying all week. "Have you heard about the credit card thing going around town?"

"Yeah, Chief. Tabor told me you had been checking some of the credit card machines around town to see if you could find a skimmer. Are we still getting reports in?"

"We are, but it seems like the problem started in Paxton and now it's leaking over into Spicetown. The sheriff's office sent me copies of their recent reports to see if we could see any common patterns." Conrad sorted the file folders into two stacks and handed one stack to Gwen.

"These are reports filed with us that mention Spicetown businesses. I need you to give each of these a follow-up call and ask them to pull their credit card statements."

"Do you need copies of their statements, Chief?"

"No, I don't need to know what was spent, just a list of every business that they used their card at for the last six weeks."

Officer Kimball nodded. "Are we looking for a common store?"

"Yes, but I'm thinking that folks are just telling us where they've been for the last few days. Some of these getups just gather a bunch of card numbers to sell the list. They don't do anything with the numbers directly. The thieves that buy the list, they're the ones making the charges. You see?"

"Yeah, Chief. That would take a few weeks to do."

"Exactly. We may find a common link with all these people, but it may have happened a month ago. It may not even be a store around here. Maybe it's some online purchase." Conrad shrugged, "but I don't really think so."

"What do you think it is?"

"Well, Sheriff Turner thinks it's one little place that we just haven't found yet, but I think the target is moving."

Gwen's eyes widened. "Do you think it's someone local?"

"I think they are planting the skimmer and moving it before we find it. That's why we need some history of their card usage. Maybe we can see dates in common where they all went to the grocery store, or they all went to a particular shop around the same day. I don't know if that can help us catch them, but at least we'll know what we're looking for."

"Gotcha, Chief. So, dates and business names for six weeks or so. I'll give them a call and see what I can get from them." Gwen walked back toward the doorway and turned around. "Has the sheriff's office actually found a skimmer anywhere in town?"

Conrad smiled. "Not that they've said. I think that's why they are leaning toward the online theory."

"They have a lot more places to check than we do." Gwen shrugged.

"True, and I'm sure they don't want to look like they can't find it, but we can't worry about that right now."

Peggy spent all morning waiting on customers in The Salty Shipper and Arlene took care of the craft side of the store. Paying for an advertisement in the Spicetown Star had worked in her favor and business was picking up. She was relieved to see traffic growing, because the first week made her nervous about her decision to pursue this venture. She hated to think the bank had been right.

"Good morning, Emily! How is your grandfather doing?" Peggy pushed a shipping label toward Emily Trammel and handed her a pen.

"He's doing well. I just ran over here to check on him since I had the day off work. How are you?"

"Doing great," Peggy said as she tapped her finger on the form. "I just need your return address up here and where it's going at the bottom in the box."

Emily nodded and leaned forward to write.

"I haven't seen Mr. Kit in a long time."

"He doesn't get out much anymore. I take him to the store, and he runs a few errands on his own, but I feel better if he waits for me to come by. I worry about him driving."

"I'm sure he loves seeing you!" Peggy peeled the edges of the label, so she could place it on the package.

"I don't know if you heard, but his debit card number was stolen. That really scared him." Emily dug into her handbag to pay Peggy.

"I did and I'm sorry to hear he's going through that, but in case you didn't know, it's happening all over town. People are reporting fraudulent charges on their credit cards."

"Yeah. The chief told me."

"It's happening in Paxton, too." Peggy caught herself before she blamed them for it, remembering Emily lived over there now.

"I made him get a credit card. If he'd been using that instead, they would have replaced the card and removed the charge right away. He doesn't want to use it, but he doesn't have a choice right now. He doesn't have anything else! I don't know what we're going to do."

Peggy didn't know what to say. She couldn't imagine what she would do if it happened to her either. "It's scary."

Emily nodded.

Peggy handed Emily her credit card back and noticed it had Otis Kittering's name on it. "There you go. It should be delivered in about 3 days. You tell Mr. Kit I said hello and have him give me a call if he needs anything,"

"I will. Thank you."

Once Emily left, Peggy picked up her phone and called City Hall. Punching in the extension for Streets and Alleys, she waited for someone to answer. "Rodney! Hi, it's Peggy Cochran at the Carom Seed Craft Corner. I know you're working, and I hate to bother you, but I need someone to replace the steel door on the back of my shop for me. Do you know anyone I could call?"

Rodney Maddox was now the supervisor of the Spicetown Streets and Alleys, but he had always been a bit of a handyman on the side. If he couldn't do it, Peggy thought he would know someone to suggest.

Rodney didn't disappoint. He told her he would send somebody around to measure the door later that day.

Next, she dialed Volker Electric and left them a voice mail message to come get their monitor and door camera. Fancy technology may be the way of things nowadays, but for her situation, it clearly wasn't the right answer.

As she walked around the counter and into the craft store, Arlene caught her eye and then let her eyes bounce off the browsing customer sending Peggy a warning to take notice. The woman was strolling the aisles, looking at merchandise, but not touching anything. She studied the products with critical appraisal, but no personal interest.

With dark brown hair to her shoulders and extra weight on her hips, the woman appeared to be in her late thirties, but dressed as if yearning to be younger. She was not a familiar face, but the shop did draw people from neighboring towns or travelers passing through, especially if they were quilters. Spicetown hosted the state's traveling quilt show each year, so quilters in southern Ohio knew about her store.

Peggy joined Arlene at the counter. "Rodney Maddox is sending someone over today to look at the back door on the shipping side. I've decided to replace it with a windowed door. I've left a message with Volker Electric to come remove their equipment."

Arlene's mouth opened, but she knew better than to question Peggy's quick action, so she nodded instead. Peggy was decisive and she rarely changed her mind. When she was done being bothered with something, she didn't look back.

After weaving down each aisle, the customer reached the end of the back row and looked down at Sully. He was reclined on his left side in a round dog bed against the wall and looked up at her without alarm. "Well, hello there, sir." The woman smiled warmly at Sully's proud display of manliness and Peggy rushed over to intervene.

"That's Sully. He's head of security, but he's on his break right now. I'm Peggy. Is there something we can help you with?"

"No, thank you. I was just looking around."

"If you embroider, the kits up front are on sale." Peggy pointed to a round table that Arlene had set up yesterday displaying framed samplers.

"Are you the proprietress of this establishment?"

The woman smiled at her own haughtiness.

"Yes, I'm Peggy Cochran. I own the Carom Seed and the Salty Shipper." Peggy pointed next door.

The woman held out her hand to shake. "I'm Regina Adkins. I've been looking at the commercial property across the way."

"Nice to meet you, Ms. Adkins." Peggy shook her hand. "This is Arlene Emery."

Arlene waved from behind the counter. "Are you looking for a place for a clothing store?"

"Yes!" Regina seemed surprised at Arlene's question.

"Sassafras?" Arlene walked around the counter.

"Why, yes! How did you know?"

Arlene hesitated, searching for the right explanation. She had said too much again.

"The small town breeze." Peggy smiled. "News is carried by the wind around here. I take it you aren't from a small town."

"No, I've never lived in a small town." Regina shook her head. "But I think they are the wave of the future. People are tired of city life and are spreading out more. I'm thinking I might like to try it."

"It's the only way to live!" Arlene said, proudly. "Spicetown would love to have you. Local businesses support each other here, and we have merchants" association that will help you." Cupping her hand around one side of her mouth she whispered, "you don't want to join the Chamber of Commerce."

"Frank and Dorothy Parish own the Caraway Cafe just down the street, and they can tell you all about the merchants' association. Most of the current businesses downtown have been here many years and are owned and run by lifelong citizens of Spicetown." Peggy's head turned when she heard the door to the Salty Shipper open.

"I'll get it." Arlene went through the doorway to the shipping side. She had been avoiding the issue, but she did need to learn how to handle these customers and now was as good as anytime.

"How quaint. You make life sound very simple."

Peggy stepped over to the cash register. "It's not easy being the sole proprietress of an establishment." Peggy could not help but smirk at that title. "But you don't feel so alone when you do it in a community like ours."

Regina nodded and smiled.

"Fennel Street will welcome you."

"Thank you. That's nice to hear." With a curt bow of her head, Regina left the store.

Chapter 16

When Peggy walked into the Caraway Cafe to pick up lunch, it was later than usual. The morning had kept Peggy and Arlene busy and seeing less of each other because they were on two different sides of the building. Neither had noticed the time until finally they realized they were hungry. Dark clouds had moved in from the west and rain was expected, so Peggy had dashed down to grab their orders before she got wet.

Cora Mae Bingham sat in her usual spot in front of the window by the sidewalk, but today she was alone, stabbing violently at a salad with a determined frown. The cafe was quiet, and Peggy wondered why she didn't wait later to eat every day. It was much more peaceful.

"Hey, Peg. Frank will have your order up any minute. Can I get you a drink?" Dorothy's demeanor matched the mood of the cafe as her lunch rush had passed.

"Hey, Dorothy. No, I don't need a drink today. No

hurry on the order. Hi, Cora." Peggy waved when she caught Cora Mae's eye and walked over to her table. "You're eating late today, too? The time got away from us. It's been a busy morning."

"Have a seat." Cora pointed to the chair across from her. "I got held up myself. Is it a full moon? It's been a crazy day."

Peggy chuckled. "It may be."

"I've had several visitors this morning. This credit card problem needs some resolution. They all come down to complain about it to me, but I can't do anything to fix it. I know the chief is working on it, but it's not a simple issue."

Peggy nodded. "I've heard about it, too. Otis Kittering's granddaughter, Emily, was in this morning, and he's the one I'm worried about most."

"Yes, everyone else got their money back. It was a little inconvenient, yes, but they weren't forced to manage the critical loss that Mr. Kit has." Cora put her napkin on the table. "Amanda is making some collection jars to put around town for him, but I don't think that will replace the funds he lost. I don't know what else to do."

"Is the chief sure that it is a credit card machine causing the problem?"

"He thinks so, but I think the sheriff feels it may be online shopping. They can't find a common business and I don't believe they've found a skimmer yet. Otis Kittering doesn't shop online though."

"No, but Emily is paying his bills, and she might have used his card to order him something."

Cora nodded.

"You know Earl Walker tried to accuse me of being the problem because Annie had shopped in my store. I don't know if he ever found out the source of his fraudulent charge." Peggy reached out to take the lunch boxes Dorothy brought to the table. "People are getting afraid to buy anything!"

"Are you talking about all those credit card frauds going on?" Dorothy swung her hip to one side and parked her hand at her waist. "People have been going in Chervil Drugs accusing them of being the problem, too. Conrad keeps checking his card machine and he hasn't found a thing wrong. I put our machine under the cash wrap, and nobody touches it unless I give it to them. I can't watch it all day!"

"Keith Hanover was another one. I don't think he uses his card much at all and he swears he's not used it in Paxton recently, but they got him, too." Cora Mae pushed her plate away from her. "The list keeps growing."

Peggy started to stand, but then rocked back in her seat to test her theory. "Oh! I almost forgot. Do you remember I asked about that empty store front by Vicki's earlier this week when the local painters were inside? Who owns that building?" Peggy looked up at Dorothy and saw a puzzled look, then looked over at Cora Mae, who was brushing imaginary crumbs from her lap.

"I don't recall, but you know they are having some interest in the building. I know they've shown it a few times lately, so maybe someone has rented it. They might have hired the painters. I think they are off finishing the Sesame Seed Sandwich Shop today. I saw them setting up out front when I drove to work. I haven't been down Tarragon Street yet though. There might be a few more buildings to do there."

"Arlene met your accountant a couple of days ago." Peggy didn't want to spread negativity unless it was requested. She hadn't actually met the man herself, but Arlene was pretty easy to get along with. If he couldn't charm her in a five-minute conversation, the man must lack people skills.

Dorothy nodded. "Yeah, the CPA. I heard he was looking."

"This morning Arlene and I met the lady who is thinking about renting the place across the street. Her name is Regina Adkins and she's got clothing stores."

Cora's eyes twinkled. "That would be so nice to have in town."

"She hasn't decided yet, but she was checking me out. If she hasn't already been here, Dot, I bet you'll see her. She's trying to get a feel for small town life. She's never lived in a small town before."

"It's not for everyone." Cora Mae huffed. She couldn't imagine why not, but she had learned that some people found redeeming qualities in the city.

"Vicki said the stores are called 'Sassafras' and they have an online site if you want to take a look. She usually goes in and sets these places up, trains everyone, and then leaves. She sounded this morning like she might want to settle down here though. Maybe she'll consider making this her home." Peggy shrugged. It was difficult to imagine, because Regina seemed to strive to be something she wasn't, but maybe there was more to her story.

"We'll have to get her in the Merchant's Association!" Dorothy squinted. "And we need to warn her about Miriam."

"Arlene already has." Peggy chuckled. "She told her not to join the Chamber of Commerce. She didn't ask us why, so Arlene didn't tell her about Miriam specifically."

"Well, we don't want to scare the poor girl off!" Cora tapped her fist on the table, and they all laughed.

Peggy stood and picked up her order. "I'll see if I can corner those painters and see what I can find out."

"Oh, I'm sure they won't know anything." Cora looked down at the table and Peggy glanced at Dorothy.

Cora always avoided eye contact when she didn't want to talk about something, and everyone except Cora Mae knew that.

"I can make a few calls and find out the owner of the building. Arlene is friends with Clyde Newman. He would know, but it's a public record. I can call the courthouse if I can't find out on the street." Peggy and Dorothy stared down at Cora Mae waiting for her reaction. Peggy wasn't desperate to know who the owner of the building was, but Cora's reluctance to tell them was the real mystery. Now she knew it was not Chief Harris that kept her from speaking freely.

"I don't think it's anyone local." Cora's face twisted with a distant thought. "It seems like it was a corporation or trust. Something like that." Tossing her hands, her expression lightened. "I just know it's not Miriam!" Cora chuckled. "The last time I looked it up I was afraid it might be."

"Well, that's a relief!" Dorothy said as she waved to Peggy when she slipped out the front door.

A light sprinkle of rain made Peggy hurry her steps, but the dark cloud engulfing Fennel Street kept her looking over her shoulder. A good storm always dampened business, so at least they might get to eat lunch without interruption.

"I'm back." Peggy waved to Arlene, who she saw was taking money at the counter in The Salty Shipper. The morning's business had given Arlene several opportunities to practice making labels and setting up shipping in the software, so her confidence was growing.

Once Arlene was able to join her on the sofa, she apologized for being late. "I ran into Dorothy and Cora Mae. The cafe lunch rush was over, so we started talking. There is something funny going on with that building across the street. Cora doesn't want to talk about it."

Arlene's head tilted in question as she took a bite of her sandwich and Peggy shared the cafe conversation with her. "Cora Mae knows who owns that building and doesn't want to talk about it. That has just made it my number one priority to find out!" Peggy laughed. "And I didn't give a whit about it before."

Arlene covered her mouth with her napkin as Peggy made her laugh with her mouth full. She was too hungry to set it aside. "Do you want me to call Clyde?"

"Yeah, I think that's the easiest place to start. If he acts funny about the question, we'll know we have to get the big guns involved."

Arlene swallowed. "The big guns?"

"I'm going to call Miriam Landry and ask her!"

Arlene gasped.

Chapter 17

"Hey, Ms. Cochran." Cecil waved when he walked in the door of The Salty Shipper. "Gary sent me over to take out your monitor." Cecil looked at the back of the store and saw the black screen. "It went out again?"

"It went out sometime yesterday afternoon and I missed my parcel post pickup. I had to close the craft store early and drive my packages over to the warehouse in Paxton before they closed."

"I'm sorry about that, Ms. Cochran. I don't understand why that keeps happening, but I think it must be the wiring. This is all new equipment."

"Well, I can't chance it. I can't close up and drive over there again. I just want it removed."

Cecil looked down at the floor and nodded. "I understand. Let me get busy and I'll get it all out of your way."

Peggy stepped back toward the pass-through doorway, so Cecil could carry his toolbox by. He had come to the front door this time instead of the back. Peggy wondered if he had tried to ring the bell at the back first and realized nothing was working.

"I appreciate it, Cecil. Just holler at me if you need anything. I'll just be next door."

Peggy stepped back over to the sofa and cleared off all the lunch debris. The street outside was dark but the cars driving down the street did not have windshield wipers on, so the storm had not arrived yet. Thunder and lightning were gathering strength as it moved closer, and Peggy saw someone jogging toward her store holding an umbrella and streaming a long white puff behind them. As they stepped under the awning, the umbrella came down and she saw Valerie Duffy's smiling face.

"Valerie is here," Peggy called out to Arlene as she pulled open the door. Sully sat up on his haunches in recognition of a kindred spirit and waited for his greeting.

Valerie struggled with her umbrella and then waved the long streamer of tulle to shake off any water. "My mom found her veil."

"Oh, good!" Peggy pushed the door shut.

"I hope I didn't drag it through the water. I should have put it in a bag, but it wasn't raining when I left home with it this morning. I just threw it in my backseat."

"A little water won't hurt it." Peggy placed it on the

fabric cutting table and spread it out.

"I told mom I didn't want to wear a veil, so she didn't get it out earlier, but then we thought you might be able to use the material in the dress somewhere." Valerie stroked her hand over the tulle. "What do you think?"

"Yeah! Sure. I can use it. I can add it to the skirt or.... Do you want a train?"

Valerie wrinkled her nose and stared at the corner of the room. "Maybe?" The lilt in her voice indicated she was answering with definite uncertainty. "Maybe a little one?"

Peggy held her index finger and thumb about two inches apart. "A little one?"

Valerie laughed. "I can't see myself dragging a big, long thing behind me, but a little tail... maybe!"

"A definite maybe. Gotcha." Peggy nodded with a sour expression and Valerie giggled. "Do you have any other solid ideas?"

"Yes! I brought some pictures."

"Come. Let's sit in the back and have a look." Peggy walked toward the back of the store and waited while Valerie petted Sully. Sully then dutifully followed Valerie to the back of the room pledging allegiance to his newfound friend. Peggy gave him an impertinent glare for his lack of loyalty and waited for Valerie to find the photos on her phone.

"Did you hear the good news?" Valerie chewed her bottom lip unsure if Peggy would be happy to hear it. "We've set a date."

"I did hear that." Peggy pinched the phone screen to enlarge one of the pictures. "Arlene told me that you and Derek were in the gas station last night when she went inside."

"Yes! We realized that the main reason we were waiting for the date was because we didn't have our own space. I'm living with Mom and Dad and he's in a tiny apartment. Getting married right away didn't make sense."

"But that's all changed?" Peggy grabbed her notebook and made a few notes with a quick drawing of the straps on the back of one of the gowns.

"Yes! Derek found us some land. We looked at it yesterday before he had to start work and it is perfect. It's closer to Paxton than Spicetown, so we'll both have a little commute, but it's only about ten minutes from my parents. He made an offer, and they accepted it!"

"That's wonderful." Peggy smiled, still not sure when the wedding date would be. "Are you going to build this year?"

"No, we're going to put a mobile home on it and then build next year. We haven't even looked at house plans or anything like that. It will take a few months to get utilities hooked up and get the mobile home ready, so we decided to get married in August, August twenty-fourth."

Peggy nodded as her mind scrambled to calculate the hours she would need to focus on the dress to be ready. "Are you wearing your hair up or down?"

Valerie frowned.

"I know that sounds like a crazy question, but if your hair is down, it might change how we do the back of the bodice."

"Oh," Valerie nodded as if she could see Peggy's reasoning. "I want it down. I've found a hair piece I want to wear. I ordered it but it hasn't yet arrived. Mom wants me to put it up with a tiara since I won't wear the veil, but I do not want to do that." Valerie shuddered.

Peggy tapped her notebook again because it helped her think and then handed Valerie back her mobile phone. "Are you okay with the top being satin or would you prefer another fabric?"

"I'm fine with satin. I don't really know much about different kinds of fabric. I trust you."

"You mentioned last time that you wanted a sweetheart neckline. Did you mean like the one your mother's dress has?"

"Her dress comes up to her neck."

"The lace does, but when you remove the lace, you have a satin sweetheart neckline underneath that shows through the lace. You didn't try it on, did you?"

Valerie mumbled something to Sully, who was making certain Valerie kept petting his head. "I didn't. I think it's too small, but I guess I didn't look at it closely enough."

"I've removed it already. Let me show you." Peggy walked to the sewing machine and picked up the satin bodice. It would still have to be remade, but at least she could make sure they were on the same page.

"I see what you mean." Valerie seemed deflated by the discovery. "Were you going to rework that?"

"No, I just wanted to be certain I understood what you wanted. We can do anything you want."

"I want straps." Valerie held her fingers about two inches apart and then traced them down her chest into a V-shape. "What if it just crossed, came to a point in the center?"

"Let me think." Peggy crossed one leg over the other and began to sketch in the notebook in her lap. "If we leave the bottom of the dress the way it is and remove the top, I can add something like this to it." Peggy showed her rough sketch to Valerie. "It can have any width strap you like over your shoulder, and it can be as high or as low in the front as you like."

"I like that! It's very sleek and simple. The bottom will be so poofy, that this will make it look a little more elegant." Valerie nodded. "Do you think I'm making a mistake keeping the bottom part? I think Mom will be crushed if I don't use some parts of it."

"I think it's a very nice thing for you to try to remake your mother's dress. All that matters is that you feel beautiful in it."

Valerie smiled.

"Would you like it to be a little less poofy? I might be able to arrange that, too."

Peggy explained her idea of a smooth back with a short train and an alternative of inserting satin between the tulle to widen the skirt but spread out the fluffiness. She agreed to do a simple mockup for her to look at next week as Arlene joined them.

"Could those satin panels be in a color? Would that look crazy? My mom would freak out, but I really like the idea of having a little color somewhere. If the satin panels under the poofy stuff were a pale peach, it might make that whole skirt pop! What do you think?"

"I think we can do anything you like! There are no rules." Peggy chuckled.

"That sounds great! My colors are light peach and green." Valerie clapped her hands, which momentarily flustered Sully. "It's all starting to feel real now!"

"The next few months will fly by!" Arlene said. "You'll have a million things to do." Arlene slipped her shoe off and rubbed her foot. This increase in business from the shipping side was putting a strain on her feet. "Start your list with comfortable shoes. You'll be dancing and standing for hours."

Valerie nodded and rubbed Sully's ears before kissing the top of his head.

"Hey, did you get your credit card problems all worked out?" Peggy cocked her head in question. "I keep forgetting to ask you."

"Oh, yeah. I just reported it, and they changed my card number. It was no big deal. Just an aggravation. I don't know whether the jewelry store ever figured out who did it or not."

Arlene sighed. "It's happened around here, too, but I heard it's much worse in Paxton. Has Derek had any problems?"

"No, but he doesn't buy much. He eats most of his meals at work and he can even get his gas at work, so he doesn't use a credit card very often. He hates to shop!"

"Most men do." Arlene rolled her eyes. "I always bought my husband's clothes. I used to tell him if it were left up to him to buy his own clothes, he'd be wearing the tablecloth."

Even Peggy had to chuckle at the mental image that projected. "Check back with me next week. We can make some big decisions then."

"Will do! See you later." Valerie gave Sully a loud kiss on the top of his head and waved as she left the store.

Peggy sat up straight up in her chair and gasped. "What time is it? We've got to watch for that package pickup!"

"Oh my gosh!" Arlene and Peggy both raced off to the shipping store.

Chapter 18

"Hello, Jason. I'm glad you stopped by." Cora Mae stood up from her desk and walked to her conference table. "I wanted to show you the latest arrangement."

Jason Marks followed Cora to the table and looked at her map of the community center's auditorium. "I'm sorry I haven't been by the last few days. I just had a little catching up to do."

"That's fine. Nothing to worry about. Amanda and I have been playing around with these tables and I've been rethinking some of the details." Cora pulled out a chair from the table and sat down.

"I think maybe I need to keep it simple, especially this first year. Sometimes I get carried away with too many ideas and try to do too much." Cora saw Amanda look through her office door and motioned for her to join them.

"This looks great, Mayor." Jason pointed at the

stage. "I thought you were putting desserts up here."

"I was, but I moved them to just below the edge of the stage in a straight line. I do still want to do a cake walk game and I thought I'd do that on the stage. Then the cakes for the event will be nearby."

Amanda chuckled. "You are going to need some explanation for this. I don't think people will know what you're talking about."

Jason smiled at Amanda. He had looked it up and sifted through the confusing information online to come to the conclusion it was a game of musical chairs crossed with bingo where you won a cake.

"I will explain it and I think you will find that more people will know about it than you think. We had them all the time downtown. Did your mother know what it was?"

Amanda reluctantly nodded. "She did. She said she walked with her mom in them when she was a kid."

Cora tossed her hands out. "There you go! I told you so. A little nostalgia is a good thing, and young people today don't know everything."

"She's still a teacher!" Jason chuckled and glanced at Amanda.

"I am and see, both of you have learned something from me. My goal has been met."

Amanda giggled.

"There is a music issue though." Cora looked

briefly up to the ceiling. "I can't remember what music we used to play, but there needs to be something playing when they walk. It should be pleasant and melodic, nothing crazy, but the beat should be the pace they take their steps with. I was thinking maybe something children would know, like a song from one of their popular shows so they would be drawn to participate, too."

"So just the food and the cake walk." Jason nodded. "Did you decide about tickets or getting an estimate on attendance? Amanda and I talked about a website where they just entered the number of people coming together and the name of a dish. We wouldn't ask anyone's name, but then we could at least get a vague idea of what to expect."

"I'm always afraid to rely on the internet. Not everyone is comfortable clicking here and there anymore. If we do something like that, we need a manual alternative, too." Cora was always mindful of the people closest to her that were uncomfortable getting online. Her friend, Violet Hoenigberg, would not know where to begin, and even Saucy was fearful of many things online.

"I think we need to enlist others to help." Amanda pulled out a chair and sat down. "People need to be needed. Attendance might be better if people felt like showing up mattered. If the Rotary Club or the Jaycees were outside cooking the meat, they would all be there. If the Girl Scouts were in charge of the cake walk music or decorations, they would want their family to come. You could ask the Ladies' Auxiliary to be servers, which would just mean they stood behind the food tables to make sure we didn't run out of anything. They would all think they were in charge." Amanda shrugged shyly because Jason and Cora Mae both stared at her. "I don't know. It was just a thought."

"You're exactly right! That's the piece I was missing all along!" Cora stood up. "I was looking for the right place to start. This is a massive undertaking and every time I thought about it, it seemed too big to imagine, and I didn't know where to start. You have solved that problem. I know exactly where to start now."

Jason decided to take a guess. "We solicit help from the community, and their response will tell us if they are interested in the idea."

"Exactly! Amanda let's think about an article in the newspaper to start. We don't want just an announcement or an ad. At this point, I think we need to explain our goals. I can get Ed to work it in on the front page when he has a slow day. We can offer responses by phone or website like we did the security detail for the 4th of July."

"I'll get started!" Amanda jumped up from her chair.

"It doesn't have to be done today, but we don't want to wait too long." Cora needed feedback. This was a lot of work to do if the citizens weren't interested. She needed her idea validated before she committed to it.

"How many can you seat with this arrangement?" Jason pointed at the map.

"About two hundred, but I'm thinking people will come and go throughout the time period, so overall we might accommodate even more."

"It sounds like an exciting event. I'm here to help with anything you need, even though my school project will be over before then."

"I'm glad to hear that. I'm sure I can use you in the planning process. It always helps me work out things if I can talk to other people about it." Cora Mae glanced at the doorway and lowered her voice. "I did want to talk to you about something else."

Jason pulled out a chair and sat down at the table.

"I wanted to let you know that Peggy Cochran and Arlene Emery are asking a lot of questions about the painters. I'm sure that means Dorothy and Vicki are involved as well. They all saw the painters inside the vacant storefront earlier this week."

Jason nodded. "I thought that was a bad idea, but...."

"They are also asking who owns that building. I tried to avoid the issue, but I finally said I thought it was a corporation or trust. I couldn't remember."

"They can look it up." Jason winced. "It's not a secret. Well, it is, and it isn't. They'll see it's a trust and they won't know who owns the trust."

"True, but if there's any clue or anything that links that trust to someone, Peggy will find it. She's like a dog with a bone when she wants to know something." Cora bared her teeth.

Jason chuckled. "Well, I'll pass that on. I appreciate the warning."

"Where are those painters now? Are they about done?"

"They are finishing Louise's Beauty Shop today and that's the last place on Tarragon Street. The Spicetown Star refused the offer. Ed Poindexter didn't want his building painted for free unless he knew who the gift came from."

"Oh, great. He's sniffing around, too, I bet."

"I just said okay and moved along. They did the Safflower Tanning Salon and Louise's. There is only one left."

"The Hart & Grace Tax Service building? It hasn't been sold yet though, has it?"

"Clyde says he thinks it will be. He's been talking to that accountant, but Jacob Hart's son won't rent it. The accountant didn't really want to buy, but he does like the building. Clyde thinks he will decide to take it because he didn't like any of the other options Clyde showed to him."

"Even with a rental offer, Jeremiah wouldn't agree?" Cora shook her head.

"No, and the building looks like an eyesore now that everyone else has newly painted storefronts."

"Oh, I'm sure it does. It's just like buying new furniture for your living room means you need new drapes, new flooring, or a fresh coat of paint. When you mix new and old, old always seems to lose."

Jason's brows knitted together as he thought that through. "Clyde feels like the guy wants to be in Spicetown, so hopefully he'll give in. He's house shopping, too."

"Fingers crossed!" Cora walked back to her desk.

"I'll check back in with you in a few days. I've got to get to work now." Jason backed toward the office door.

"Tell Dot I said hello!"

Conrad Harris followed Canine Officer Briscoe down the hallway toward the dispatch cubicle. "Good morning, Kimball. Did you get anything back on those credit cards yet?"

"Morning, Chief. I've got a couple bringing in their statements today, but I got three that gave me a list on the phone. I put a copy of the report on your desk."

Conrad nodded and looped Briscoe's leash on the hook by the door. "Where's Georgia?"

"I think she's in the break room."

"Did any of the lists have a common business?"

"Chervil's Drugs." Gwen shrugged with regret. "The hits were not during the same week, and we know Chervil's machines are clean now."

"It makes me think they are planting the skimmers and removing them before they can be discovered."

Gwen's blank expression showed uncertainty. "They did all have online purchases on them, too."

"The same website?"

"No." Gwen saw the gaping holes in her theory. "But it does show they do shop online."

Officer Georgia Marks, Jason's mom and weekday dispatcher walked back to her cubicle with a cup of coffee in her hand. "Hey, Chief. Good morning, Briscoe." Briscoe had curled up in his favorite spot under the counter in the dispatch cubicle. It was dark under the counter for maximizing nap time yet kept him at the center of all the action.

"Morning, Georgia. Have you checked in on your neighbor, Otis? Has he heard anything from the bank?"

"No, Chief. They told him it could be up to six weeks before they complete their investigation, but he did say they changed his account number and gave him a temporary credit, so he has some spending money."

"I don't want him to miss his light bill or rent payment and not tell anybody he's in a bind."

"I'll keep an eye on him, Chief. Jason goes over every few days and looks in on him, too. I think he owns his house, and we can make sure he has food. I'll check on him about his utilities."

Conrad nodded with a grunt as he shuffled his feet when he turned to go back to his office. He knew Mr. Kit wouldn't want anyone making a fuss, but Cora Mae needed to do that thing she always did to take care of this. He'd have to remember to remind her!

Chapter 19

Peggy opened both stores that morning and put Sully in his crate. Arlene was going to be running late because she had a doctor's appointment, and Peggy had a shipment of her own to pack up. She'd received some items she wanted to return and was delighted to know it would be easy to do now that she was the town shipper.

Peggy dragged the large box of quilt batting across the floor of the craft store and around the counter on the shipping side, leaving the flaps open so she could include her return paperwork. When she spun around looking for the tape dispenser, the chime on the door had her spinning back the other way.

"Hi, Andy!"

Andy Gentry, Rodney Maddox's stepson, smiled. "Hey, Ms. Cochran. I haven't been in here before. It's pretty cool."

"Thank you. It's a little empty so far, but we're still

working on the decoration part."

"Rodney sent me over to measure your door." Andy waved the tape measure he held in his palm.

"Oh!" Peggy jumped. "It's the door back here. I need a steel door like this except I want a window in it. You know, the kind that has metal wire built inside the glass, so it doesn't break easily? I want to be able to see out, but I don't want anyone breaking in."

"Whoa. I better write all that down."

"Do you need some paper?" Peggy looked under the counter for a pen.

"Nah, I'll just put it in my phone. How big a window do you want?"

"Face size?" Peggy chuckled. "I don't care if it's the whole top half as long as it's secure."

Andy nodded as his thumbs flew across the phone display. Peggy never understood how people could type with their thumbs.

"You see, the problem is that I need to be able to see the package pickup guy when he comes to the door. I need a doorbell that works, too."

"He can probably do that for you if he can find you a door. That's why he sent me down here, so he could check around and see if the door was in stock anywhere."

"That sounds good." Peggy's head turned when the bells on the craft store door jingled. "I've got to go. Holler if you have any questions."

Andy nodded and turned toward the door as Peggy shuffled to the other side.

"Morning, Ms. Walker! How are you today?" Peggy was relieved to see Annie Walker return to her store. She was afraid Earl wouldn't let her shop there anymore after the credit card issue.

"Good morning, Peggy. I just stopped in for a little more of that satin ribbon. You know the tiny, tiny ribbon that I bought last time. I'm using it in my cross stitch to box in the design before I frame them. I think it's prettier than matting and it's just something different."

"It sounds really pretty! You'll have to bring one by the store so I can see it. If you decide you want to make some to sell, we are going to be putting up handmade items next door for sale. You might make a little pocket change."

"Sometimes I like to try something new and change out the little pictures I have around the house. It brightens things up. I should have brought one with me. I'll try to remember to do that next time." Annie handed Peggy two bolts of 1/16th inch ribbon, one in a light blue and another in a pale yellow. "I think two yards of each should cover it."

Peggy took the spools to the fabric table and cut the lengths Annie needed, writing up a charge ticket and walking up to the cash register. "Can I get you anything else?"

The shipping door opened and chimed.

"No, that's all I need." Annie walked toward the counter and stopped to touch the different fabrics.

Peggy quickly looked around the doorway into the shipping side and saw a man waiting. Holding up a finger, she said, "I'm checking someone out over here, but I'll be right with you."

"No problem."

The man looked familiar, but Peggy wasn't certain why. Andy seemed to have measured the door and left already, so she took Annie's credit card for payment and held the door for her. Earl was probably waiting outside in the car.

As soon as the door shut, Peggy rushed to the other side. "I'm sorry for the wait. What can I do for you?"

"I just need to get this package sent." The man placed a small square box on the counter. "Can you tape it up for me?"

Peggy noticed paint on the man's hands and then it dawned on her. "Aren't you the painter that helped with my sign?"

The man chuckled. "Yeah, that's me. I guess it's still doing okay?"

"I thought you looked familiar, but it took me a minute. Yes, it is doing fine. I appreciate your help. I wasn't sure how I was going to get it fixed."

"No problem. It just took a minute."

Peggy slid the label across the counter with a pen. "I just need you to fill out the top of the form with the to and from. I'm going to put a little packing in here, so the box doesn't rattle, and I'll tape it up for you." The tiny box held a black plastic part that didn't look like anything Peggy had seen before. It was round with a rubber gasket inside and a small plastic piping attached.

The man picked up the pen and began to write as Peggy prepared the box for shipping.

"How is the painting around town going? Are you guys about done?" Peggy weighed the box.

"Yeah, there's just a couple left."

"I noticed you were over there painting the inside of the vacant store. A couple of the merchants have asked about it. Are you taking on extra painting around town while you're here?"

"Nah, we just paint what we're told to. Is this the box where the other address goes?" He pointed at the larger box.

"That's where you'll want to put the address you are sending it to."

"Okay." The man slid the label back to her and handed her a twenty-dollar bill.

Peggy gave him his change and wished him a good day, although he never lifted his eyes to meet hers. He clearly wasn't in a sharing mood. Sticking the label on the box, she saw the sender was listed as Joe Englewood with an address in Ingram, Pennsylvania, and the box was going to a painting company in Pittsburgh, Pennsylvania.

As Joe the painter walked out of The Salty Shipper front door, Harvey Salzman slipped in. "Hey, Peggy."

"How are you, Saucy?" Peggy didn't see anything in Saucy's hands, so she assumed he was just stopping in to visit. When the weather was nice, Saucy always checked in with the shop owners on Fennel Street when he was out on his walk.

"I'm great! I had to stop in and look around. I haven't been in The Salty Shipper yet and I wanted to take a look around. This seems like it's the perfect space for a shipping store."

"It's really small, so you can't do too many things here. Do you want to come next door and take a break? I've got coffee made if you'd like some."

"No, thank you. I just popped in for a look around. Did you see that guy that just left?" Saucy tossed his hooked thumb over his shoulder and lowered his voice to be discreet. "He's one of those store painters from Pittsburgh."

"Yeah, I didn't recognize him at first, but then I realized he was the guy that straightened my sign out front."

"Oh, yeah." Saucy pointed his finger at Peggy, remembering that morning. "He and his buddy work for that mystery money man in Pittsburgh that's helping everyone fix up their place. Well, I guess you knew that since they helped you with this store, didn't they?"

"I have no idea who they are. I got my loan through them to buy this shop, but it was just some corporate name. How do you know?"

"I have big ears!" Saucy pulled on his earlobe and grinned. "I hear them talking in the bakery every morning. They go in there for coffee before they start painting."

"I asked the guy that was just in here about the painting he did inside the store across the street. I didn't think they were supposed to be painting the interior and I wondered if he was taking on extra painting jobs while he was in town, but he said he just does what he's told."

"They weren't too happy about that job." Saucy nodded his head. "They're outside painters, but they got a call to do it, so they did."

"I know someone is thinking about renting it. Do you know who owns the building?"

"Those money people own that building! And that lady who looked at it, is buying it!"

"Are you sure?" Peggy scowled. Regina Adkins had seemed undecided about even opening a business in Spicetown. "Are you talking about the lady with the clothing stores?"

"Yep, that's her. She looked at it to rent, but then

the owner suggested she buy the building. I guess they wanted to get rid of it, and I think they gave her a good deal, but she asked for some work to be done over there first. It looks like the painters are getting stuck doing that stuff."

"Saucy, do you have any idea who these mystery money people are? Or why they want to invest in Spicetown?" Peggy had not always been a conspiracy theorist, but the drama with the plastics manufacturing people this year had made her suspicious of big business.

"Not a clue." Saucy shook his head. "I'm not even sure these painters know. They seem to be just taking orders from a supervisor. I've heard them on the phone with him, some guy named Joe."

Maybe the guy that just left her store was sending that package to his boss. "Hmm, do you know if anything is happening with the old Hart & Grace Building? It hasn't been painted yet. Arlene said she met some guy that looked at it, but he wanted to rent, and Jacob's son wants to sell it."

Saucy rubbed his hands together and grinned mischievously. "I think a plan is afoot to remedy that. I think those mystery money people might buy it from Jeremiah Hart and then rent it to the newcomer. I know they are floating that idea around because the painters are grumbling about having to paint the inside of that place, too."

Peggy smirked and cocked her head. "It would make sense, I mean, if these mystery people are genuinely wanting Spicetown to prosper."

Saucy's bushy eyebrows came together to form a line. "Do you think there's something else going on here?"

Peggy sighed and shrugged. "I hope not."

Chapter 20

"Sorry I'm so late." Arlene pushed the door shut and slipped her purse on a shelf beneath the cash register. "They were running behind this morning."

"What did you think of the new doctor?" Spicetown now had a new primary care physician that was permanently claiming the local Urgent Care facility as her own. For too long, Spicetown had been limited to rotating traveling doctors and students who kept the small clinic open. Dr. Sachs had completed her residency in Paxton and then claimed Spicetown as her permanent home. The reviews were still out.

"She seemed nice. It was just a routine check-in visit, so I didn't talk to her long. She's very pretty."

Peggy shrugged. The encounter would need to be pretty bad for Arlene to say anything else. "You missed Saucy. He dropped in to check out the other side."

"Did you tell him we plan to have a consignment

wall in there?"

"No, we got sidetracked talking about town stuff. One of the painters came in right before him, but I did find out some interesting information."

Peggy filled her in on Saucy's scoop and then Arlene came over to sit down. Peggy had notepapers scattered all over the sofa cushions and was sitting off to one side.

"What's all this?"

"Ah, just crazy notes I've made. I was trying to piece them all together into one sheet. I've been trying to keep track of the card skimmer stories and where everyone shopped. There has to be something in common with all of them. I'm just overlooking it somehow."

Arlene jumped up when the shipping door rang. "I'll get it."

Peggy had drawn a chart on a large sheet of paper and listed the victims across the top boxes. Then she listed the businesses they had visited down the first column. Going through her notes, she put a check in the boxes where the victim and business intersected. She had gone over her notes twice now and everything she knew about was listed, but there was no business row with checks all the way across. What was she missing?

"Peg, Andy is here with the door. He's going to drive around back and drop it off. Do you want to look at it and make sure it's what you want?"

"Yeah, I'm coming." Peggy gathered her notes and shoved them in the back of her notebook before walking to the back door.

"Hi, Andy! Wow! This is great. It's perfect." Peggy stood back and looked at the door in the back of his truck. "The window is much bigger than I expected, but I see it has security wire in it. This is exactly what I need."

"Great! I'm going to just set it inside the back door, so you have it. I'm not sure who is coming by to hang it for you, but it should be in the next few days. We got lucky and they had it in stock." Andy's friend jumped out of the passenger side of the truck and helped Andy remove the door from the truck bed.

"That's great." Peggy held the door open for them. "Thank you, Andy and tell Rodney thanks, also." Andy waved and the two young men jumped back into the truck and drove away.

Peggy returned to the craft side to find Cora Mae sitting on the sofa with Arlene studying Peggy's grid of notes. "Hi, Cora."

Cora jumped and turned around toward Peggy as she approached. "Arlene was showing me this chart of businesses that you put together. You should show this to the chief."

"Oh, I'm sure he's already done the same thing. I was just consolidating my notes and trying to see if there was a pattern. It's bugging me that this doesn't make sense unless there's something I don't know." Peggy sat down in the chair next to the sofa, and Sully waddled over for a scratch behind the ear.

"Something you don't know, like what?" Cora Mae scooted forward in her seat. She rarely sat on the sofa because her feet didn't touch the ground.

"They must have gone somewhere else they are forgetting to mention, or the skimming wasn't recent. Maybe the card number was stolen a month ago and just not used until now. That's too big a time frame for people to remember where they've gone." Peggy's hand slapped on her leg. This was frustrating her.

"That's true." Arlene nodded. "There are just too many variables and pieces missing. We aren't seeing the entire picture. What have you heard from the chief?"

"Not much." Cora placed the paper on the table. "I know he's been asking them to print out their credit card statements or bring him a list. He may be doing the same thing you are. I don't know specifically, but it's still happening."

"Did someone new get hit?" Peggy sat forward ready to grab her pen. Another lead might tie everything together.

"Not here in Spicetown," Cora said. "The chief said the county is still getting reports though."

"After Emily stopped in to ship something, it

reminded me that you mentioned a donation jar for Otis Kittering, but I've never gotten one. Is he doing okay?"

"We were going to put out donation jars for the Spicetown Beautification Fund, too, but that's all been put on hold. I think the chief is afraid to add to the problems right now. He doesn't want people to have more of their hard earned money stolen." Cora had been disappointed she couldn't implement Jason's donation idea, but she could see Conrad's point.

"I noticed Emily paid with a credit card in Otis' name, so I guess that is how he is getting by for now." Peggy crossed her legs and looked down at her hands in her lap. "I've been thinking that I probably need cameras on both cash wraps. Ted Parish told me he had them installed at Chervil Drugs."

"I guess that's just the way of the future everywhere, but it makes me sad to hear that. I never thought I'd see that in Spicetown." It also confirmed Cora's belief that her time as mayor was coming to an end.

"The town is growing!" Arlene tried to lighten the mood. "We have new people moving here, new businesses interested in opening, and new homes being built, all because they want the life we have. If we need these things to set boundaries and reinforce our values to the community, then I can only hope it keeps things status quo. I want to feel safe, but I also want to feel I'm among family."

Cora and Peggy nodded their heads in agreement, and Cora Mae pushed up from the sofa to stand. "If you don't mind, I'll tell the chief about the list you've made. He might want to take a look at it."

"Sure." What Peggy really wanted was a look at those credit card statements.

"He's probably waiting for me now at the cafe. Have a good day, ladies. I must be off!"

Arlene chuckled at Cora Mae's dramatic exit and Peggy sighed. The shipping side had been more demanding than she had anticipated, and although the day was only half over, she was tired. She wasn't complaining about the robust business. She only made a couple of dollars in handling charges for each customer, so she needed the volume, but she might need to hire someone full time for that side. Cameras would definitely be needed then.

"What do you think about cameras on the cash registers?"

Arlene shrugged. "I guess it's probably a good idea. I can't imagine there being a hold-up in here, but I never hesitated to swipe my credit card before either."

"Well, this morning I was checking out Annie Walker when the painter came in for shipping. I told him I'd be a minute and it wasn't long, but he was over there by himself. He could have emptied that cash register and left if he'd wanted to. I'm sure the same will happen on this side, too."

"That's true. We can't be everywhere."

"At the last Merchants' Association meeting, when Cora told everyone about the donation jars she would be passing out, Bryan Stotlar said something about people stealing them. Out at the plant nursery, he doesn't keep someone on the cash register all the time, and he was concerned the jars might walk off on their own."

"He gets a lot of business from all over, too. It's not just Spicetown people." Arlene didn't like to think anyone around here would do that.

"A camera on the counter would at least catch that kind of thief as well as someone trying to tamper with a credit card machine."

"When I finished with the doctor and went to the counter to pay, I noticed the girl took my credit card from me to swipe. They don't have a unit on the counter like most places do. I never gave it a thought before, but that may be what everyone needs to do to keep someone from tampering with it."

"If you can trust your employees." Peggy stood up and looked out the front window. "Are you getting hungry? I thought I might take Sully for a quick walk down the block and then lunch."

"Sounds good."

Chapter 21

Peggy saddled up Sully in his new bright yellow harness with the shiny silver clasps. Arlene had ordered it online when she saw Sully was quickly outgrowing his previous walking vest. She thought Arlene felt guilty for Sully being a burden to Peggy, but he really wasn't. Peggy liked to gripe about him, but it was nice to have someone to talk to at home, even if he didn't talk back—especially since he didn't talk back.

Once out the front door. Sully waddled down the sidewalk with a proud strut as if he was a prize fighter showing off his new attire, and the metal rings on the harness jingled with every bouncing step he took. Peggy waved to Cora Mae and Conrad, who were seated in their usual place in front of the window in the Caraway Cafe and stopped at the end of the block in front of Chervil Drugs. Turning to cross Fennel Street, Peggy saw someone standing in front of the empty Hart & Grace

Tax Service building that looked like Grace Keslar.

"Mrs. Keslar?" Peggy pulled back on Sully's leash after they reached the other side of the road and waited to see if the woman turned around. She usually walked back down Fennel Street to the bakery before crossing the street again to go to her store. Sully didn't tolerate long walks, especially when it was warm outside.

Grace turned around and waved, so Peggy tugged Sully to cross again to Clove Street, so they could go say hello.

"Hello, Peggy! How are you?"

"I'm fine."

"And who is this?" Grace looked down at Sully's drooling face.

"This is Sully, my dog. I was just letting him get a little exercise before lunch." Peggy looked up at the Hart & Grace building. It looked dingy compared to the others with their new paint jobs. Jacob Hart had owned the building and the business, but since his death it had been vacant. His only heir, his son Jeremiah, didn't live in Spicetown. "Are you thinking of buying Jacob's building? I know his son would like to sell it."

"I'm waiting for Clyde Newman from Red Pepper Realty. He's going to show me the inside."

"So, you are thinking of buying it?"

"Clyde just asked me to consider it. He has a young man that's interested in renting and Jacob's son won't agree to it. Clyde thought maybe I'd like to buy it and rent it as an investment. I don't really need another business that requires my time."

"Maybe this would take care of itself though or Clyde might manage the rental end for you." Peggy was always amazed at how much Grace already did at her age. Running the Irenic Wellness Spa mostly took care of itself, but all those people staying at her house seemed like a maddening inconvenience. Grace appeared to enjoy the chaos it created though.

"That's what he implied, but I don't usually invest in real estate. I'm concerned it's an old building sitting vacant for some time now. I don't want to buy something needing me more than I need it, if you know what I mean." Grace smiled.

"Yes, older structures can become money pits. I did hear there was an accountant wanting some office space to rent. Arlene met him when he was looking at the space next to the bakery."

"Mr. Miniken, yes. I haven't met him, but Clyde told me he was not interested in purchasing. That in itself gives me pause." Grace raised her eyebrows. "What does he know that I do not?"

"It may be that he just doesn't have the money to buy it. Arlene said he's only interested in part-time work. I assumed he was retiring from his regular career."

"Perhaps." Grace cocked her head coyly to the side. "Although if anyone were to manage their finances well, you would think it would be an accountant, wouldn't you?"

Peggy smiled. "Yes, I guess you would."

"If he doesn't see it as a wise investment, why should I?"

Peggy nodded. "I didn't know his name. Arlene just met him briefly. Do you know where he's from?"

Grace swallowed. "It seems that is a bit of a mystery. Clyde didn't know and I asked Stanley to check on it. He has some magical connection to the cyberworld that I'll never understand." Grace waved her hands broadly to exaggerate Stanley's wisdom while rolling her eyes back, and Peggy chuckled.

"But Stanley said he couldn't find a single thing on him and that's saying something. Maybe I misunderstood his name, or we are spelling it wrong, but Stanley can always find something."

"Have you mentioned this to Chauncey?" Peggy laughed when her comment made Grace giggle with glee. Grace had a big, beautiful cat named Chauncey, who she claimed was the true sleuth at the mansion. He always had every mystery figured out before she did.

"That's a splendid idea! I'll be sure and get him on the case as soon as I get home."

"I see Clyde pulling in over there." Peggy pointed

to the parking lot on the side of the building. "We need to get back to the store. Good luck with your tour!"

"Jason! Come in." Cora Mae waved Jason Marks into her office. He usually came by before he began work at the cafe, so she was surprised to see him at the end of the day.

"Afternoon, Mayor. I hope it's okay that I stopped by."

"Of course! Have a seat."

"I just wanted to drop this off." Jason handed her a few typed pages and pulled a chair over to sit across from her desk. "I wrote something about the card skimmers, and I was going to take it to the Spicetown Star to see if they would print it. I thought you might want to look it over before I do that."

"Splendid." Cora put her reading glasses on and dropped her head.

"I did some research and it's really quite involved. There are several different kinds, but my mom talked to the chief about it, and he gave her some suggestions about what we should tell people to look for."

Cora would have to read it through completely but

was pleased with how it began. "I'll take a look and Amanda can walk it over to the paper on Monday. We'll put your name on it, of course, but it might get published faster if it's submitted from this office." She was afraid they would set it aside and ignore it if Jason took it in on his own.

"Great! If you want me to change anything or add anything, just let me know. I can give Amanda a call on Monday and see if there is anything you need me to do."

"That will be fine. The chief doesn't really have anyone to write these types of things for him, and I'd like to see his office have more of a voice. The way things are going today, everyone needs to be more wary than they once were. These suggestions are always welcome."

"I've been waiting around to see what the Star was going to say about the credit card scandal, but I haven't seen anything."

Cora Mae sighed and removed her glasses. "We often have to feed information to them. They lean towards publishing the negative and dramatic more than the thought provoking and educational. It's a conversation I've had many times with the editor, Ed Poindexter. I guess news reporters seek to awe their readers rather than inform them nowadays."

"The paper might grow in size and popularity if it were a bit more positive and instructional." Jason shrugged. "Maybe I'm wrong. People do love juicy stories."

"I think it can be both. It just seems we have to help them out with it."

"Oh," Jason held up his finger. "One more thing. I got a shipping notice on the first of the park benches. I'm having them delivered to the city garage. There is some assembly required but I don't think it's much. They can probably do it at the site before they bolt them down."

"Wonderful! I want as many in place as possible before our July festivities. The donated bench from the Spicer family can be installed at the same time. I'll make sure Rodney is aware they will be arriving next week."

"Okay, Mayor." Jason stood up. "I know our time is coming to an end soon, and I wanted to tell you that I've really enjoyed seeing a part of what you do to run this town. It's more involved than I ever imagined, but it's inspiring to see the thought and care that goes into all of your decisions."

Cora's shoulders stiffened. "But why is it ending? Does it have to?"

Jason lowered his head with a bashful smile. "My observation period is up and I'm working on my thesis now."

"I'm sure that will keep you busy but know that you are always welcome to brainstorm with me anytime and I'll be counting on your help at the Thanksgiving event. I'll need your advice to pull that one off!"

"You've got it! I'll always make time to help with anything you have going on. Just let me know what you need."

"I'll hold you to that! Good luck on your thesis." Cora winked as Jason waved goodbye.

Chapter 22

Peggy unlocked the back door for Arlene and then led Sully inside the craft shop. Saturdays were busy on Fennel Street, so Arlene tried to park in back near the alley, so she didn't use up a parking place meant for shoppers. It was nearly time to open, so Arlene secured her purse and turned the lights on in the lobby while Peggy squatted down to put Sully in his crate.

"Peggy!" Arlene's raspy whisper startled her. "You have customers waiting out front on the shipping side!"

"You don't have to whisper, Arlene. They can't hear you." Peggy chuckled.

"I know, but can you believe that? Isn't that wonderful? This business is really in demand. Most places that open up sit empty because everyone's afraid to be the first to snoop around. You've got people lined up at the door! This was a brilliant idea you had."

"I wish that were true," Peggy said as she pushed

herself back to a standing position. "But I think it's just temporary. Since the pickup spot closed, I think folks have just been sitting on shipments because they had to go to Paxton to drop them off. It's too far to drive for just that reason, so they were waiting on the next time they drove over there for something else."

"Still, I think Saturdays will be your busy day over there."

"Yeah, and I told Rodney that he could send someone to hang the door today. I hope that doesn't cause a problem." Peggy walked over to the shipping side and looked out the front plate-glass window. "It's just a couple of people."

Arlene looked around the doorway. "I see another walking up. Let me know if you need help with anything."

Peggy turned the lock on the door and flipped the closed sign to open. "Come in." Rushing back to get the computer turned on and the cash register open, she took her first customer for the day and the first few hours flew by.

When she finally had a lull in business, it was almost noon, and she was fighting her cravings for a Sesame Subs' sandwich when she heard a knock at the back door. The sound initially left her frozen in fear. Not knowing who was on the other side of the door had become what all her nightmares were made of since she was stalked by the rich and crazy a few months ago.

Arlene's head popped through the doorway. "Do you want me to get that?"

"No thanks. I'm finished with the customers now." Arlene's words had jolted her back to reality. "It's probably the person Rodney sent to hang the door."

"Oh, yes! That's good timing. At least it's quiet right now."

Peggy pulled open the door and a small, freckled man with rumpled hair smiled back.

"Hey there, I'm Fig!"

Peggy kept her hand tightly on the doorknob and stared warily.

"Darryl Figgins. I work for Mrs. K. Mrs. Keslar, out at the mansion. You probably don't remember me, but you used to come out there on Tuesdays for that ladies' group."

Peggy eased the door wider. He did look slightly familiar, and she did go to Grace's house every Tuesday throughout the winter for the knit and crochet group they called Tuesday Tea. "I'm Peggy Cochran."

"Oh, yeah. I know. I remember you."

"Did Mrs. Keslar send you?" Peggy had not mentioned anything to Grace this morning about needing help.

"No, Rodney. Rodney Maddox. He calls me if he needs some extra work. I do a little of this and a little of that, but not a lot of any one thing. It's my day off at the mansion, so I said I'd come by and hang your door, if that's okay."

"Uh," Peggy stammered and looked at Arlene. "This is Arlene. She works here, too."

"Hello Mr. Figgins. Do you have someone coming to help you with this?" Arlene stepped up to the shipping counter and leaned against it. "I think the door is really heavy."

"You can call me Fig. Nah, it should be okay. Can I come in?"

Peggy stumbled back and pulled the doorknob with her. "Yes, I'm sorry. Please, come in."

Fig picked up his toolbox and turned sideways to enter, giving Peggy a wondering side-eyed glance. "This the door?"

"Yes, it is, and the new one is leaning over there near the corner." Peggy pointed and backed further away until she reached the counter. "Do you need anything from us?"

"No, ma'am. I don't want to keep you from your work."

"We'll get out of your way then." Peggy pulled on Arlene's arm. "We'll be right next door."

"Such a tiny little man." Arlene whispered. "I don't

know how he can lift that door."

"I wish Rodney would have given me a name so I wouldn't have been so surprised. I just thought it would be Rodney and his stepson or Herman Latley. Herman works for Rodney at the city garage, and he does handyman jobs around town."

"Do you remember this guy from Mrs. Keslar's?"

"Vaguely. Maybe. There was a little guy out working in the yard or around the outside of the house when I was there, but I never paid any attention."

"Well, he knew you!" Arlene snickered. "He might be interested in hanging those shelves for you for the consignment items. Jenny Coleman brought in an afghan earlier." Peggy had seen Jenny in the shipping line waiting her turn. She thought she wanted to ship the afghan somewhere, but when she got to the counter, she said she was here for consignment, so she sent her to the other side to Arlene.

"Did the new forms work out? Did she set a price?"

"Yes, we got it all taken care of, and she said she is working on a cross stitch kit now that she thinks she'll bring in. It's a set of three that go together. Jenny does a lot of quilting, too, so maybe she'll bring one of those in someday."

"We do need to get those shelves built. I had planned to do that myself. I can hang shelf brackets, but I need to find the time to go to the hardware store. I still haven't decided what to do about cameras. I need to ask Ted Parish who installed his at Chervil Drugs. I know his are up and running."

Peggy talked Arlene into Sesame Subs for lunch and placed an order over the phone before the banging began. Peeking around the doorway, it appeared that Fig was at war with the hinges on the old steel door and removing it may prove a bigger challenge than hanging the new door.

"I think he needs some help." Peggy felt sorry for him and ashamed of the smile that she couldn't stifle.

"I keep having this mental image of the door coming loose, falling inside the store, and flattening him like a roadrunner cartoon." Arlene's giggle almost turned into an unladylike snort. "I know that's awful of me."

Peggy looked away to hide her laughter and shook the crazy image from her mind when the front door sounded on the shipping side. "I'll get that."

"Okay, I'll go get our lunch. I think I'll drive down since I'm parked in the alley." Arlene didn't like to lose her parking place out front during the workweek, but Sesame Subs was about a two-block walk.

Peggy nodded before walking through the doorway. "Sorry for the noise." Peggy glanced back at Fig. "How can I help you?"

Peggy handled the shipping transaction quickly

and left just as Fig turned on a drill. Everything to do with that back door was cursed! Suddenly, she realized that Rodney had not mentioned the old door. Would that be taken away for her? She couldn't possibly lift it herself. She went back to the shipping counter and waited for a break in the chaos.

"Excuse me. Are you taking the old door with you today? I didn't think to ask Rodney about that when we set this up."

Fig's head whipped around with a wild-eyed stare as if he had forgotten there was anyone else around. "Oh, I don't know. He didn't tell me. Do you want it hauled off?"

"I do. It will just be in my way here and I don't have any use for it right now."

"Let me call Rodney and see. I bet he'll want it. He collects all types of stuff like that and reuses it when other people's things need fixin'."

Peggy waited while Darryl placed the call and wished for Arlene to hurry back.

"Yep, he said he'll drop by in about an hour and get the door for you." Darryl dropped his mobile phone into his shirt pocket and started to return to his work, but saw Peggy was still standing at the counter. "It looks like your new business is doing good."

"So far, but we've only been open a few days."

"It's tough being in business nowadays. Growing

up, my uncle ran a hardware store in Red River and seemed to live the good life. I worked for him when I was young. Now, those little stores seem to be struggling."

"Yes, many of them have closed. It isn't easy."

"What made you want to replace this door if you don't mind me asking? It's pretty sturdy and it's up there real good. Did you just want a window?"

"I tried to have a camera and doorbell installed but it wouldn't work consistently, and I missed my delivery pickup driver. I need to know when the guy comes for the packages, and when I couldn't count on the technology, I decided I just need to be able to see out."

"Doing it old school!" Fig laughed.

"Yes." Peggy smiled when Fig wiggled his shoulders. "I'm still considering adding more cameras inside, especially since there is so much going on with credit card machines around here now, but I haven't had time to arrange that yet."

"I got my credit card number swiped back a few months ago, February, I think. I'm pretty sure I know right where it happened, but they ain't got no cameras there."

"Did you tell the owners?"

"I did. They're a nice couple and they felt really bad about it, but I got it fixed up okay after making a bunch of calls to the company. I told them, 'don't even send me a new card. I don't need this headache'." Fig chuckled.

"Did someone tamper with their credit card machine?" Peggy looked down and pushed the buttons on her machine. The chief had told her the buttons should be firm, not spongy.

"Oh, I don't know. I just figure an employee stole the number, but I know they can do some kind of thing on gas pumps to steal your number when you use your card."

"Did that happen in Spicetown?"

"No, out on the highway a bit, just past the road to Mrs. Keslar's place there's a little store called Slim Pickens. Now I don't mean to speak bad of them. I know Slim and Edie. They're fine people. I know they didn't do it, but they do hire help here and there. I suspect it was one of them that did it."

Peggy nodded. Why did that name keep popping up? She hadn't been to Slim Pickens' store in ages. When she heard Arlene yell out that she'd returned, she turned back to the craft store ready for lunch.

Chapter 23

Business for the shipping store quieted after lunch and Rodney stopped in to help Fig finish up. The craft shop had a few new faces stop in for a walk around, and Arlene told them all her great ideas, loading them up with her imagination. Peggy had never guessed Arlene would be so good at this job when she hired her.

Peggy priced some shelving online, deciding it might be cheaper to hire someone to stand in The Salty Shipper and just hold the products up, and then returned to Valerie's dress makeover. The pale peach satin was on order, and she was taking out seams in the skirt to be ready for the panels when it arrived. She had already cut out the bodice in white satin but would probably put that together at home where the only interruptions were Sully's snoring and her neighbor's obsession with mowing his yard every other day.

Peggy glanced up when the bells on the craft door

jingled and had to look twice to confirm that Chief Conrad Harris was standing in her store. He wasn't a crafter, so his presence meant business, but she was always taken aback when she saw him out of uniform.

"Hi, Chief!" Arlene pushed the credit card machine toward the edge of the counter. "Are you here to check the machines?"

"Haven't you been checking them every day? I showed you how to do it."

Arlene's forehead wrinkled. "I think that's Peggy's department." Arlene was afraid to take the box apart because she might not be able to get it back together.

Conrad chuckled and used the leather folder in his hand to point at Peggy sitting in the chair by the sofa. "I just came by to talk to Peggy."

Arlene waved him toward the back and smiled.

Conrad stood at the end of the coffee table and stared at Peggy with his hands at his hips.

"Have a seat." Peggy thought his expression implied he was here to scold her, but she didn't think she'd done anything... recently. He'd made her promise to stop following people around and she had. "What can I do for you?"

"The mayor tells me you have been keeping notes on what you know about the shopping habits of the credit card victims." Conrad opened his leather folder on the couch and paused to look up at Peggy for a response.

"I have tried to jot a few things down as I hear them." Peggy's eyes turned to the corner of the room and then she remembered the chief explaining to her how he could tell how someone is lying. "I was just looking for a common business."

Conrad nodded. "I have done the same. What was your conclusion?"

"There isn't one!" Peggy turned her palms up and dropped her hands in her lap. "I may not have enough information, in fact, I'm sure I don't, but I didn't find any one location that everyone had in common."

"Usually, skimmers target a single business. They leave the skimmers in place until they are found because it's risky to remove them."

"That makes sense. Do you think these skimmers are being removed or moved to other businesses?"

"It's possible." Conrad shut his folder. "Do you mind if I take a look at your notes? You might have heard something I didn't."

Peggy placed the wedding dress skirt in an empty chair and reached for her grid on the sewing machine. "It's just a table where I tried to keep track of the different places that were mentioned. I was hoping to see a pattern."

Conrad took the paper and slipped his reading glasses on to study the list. "I see you wrote a note on the edge that mentions gas with a question mark."

"Yes, I thought it odd that only one or two mentioned getting gas. I think people forget about it because you do it all the time. I always thought most of the skimmers were on gas pumps. That's what you always hear about."

"It's still a pretty popular choice." Conrad saw reports that Paxton would find one here and there every so often, but not a rash of victims without a source, like they had right now. Paxton had state highway traffic running north and south through town, so it made their businesses on the main road a tempting target. "I have their credit card statements and most of them do show buying gas, but I still didn't find them to use a common station."

"I'm sorry it's no help. I really just did it to organize my own thoughts. I was hoping putting it down on paper would unclutter my mind." Peggy huffed. "It really only created more questions."

Conrad took a picture of Peggy's grid with his phone and returned it to her. "While I'm here, I guess I'll check your machines. Kimball was working on that last week, but I think she only got as far as the bakery. Have you looked at them?"

Peggy tossed the grid back on the sewing machine and followed Conrad as he walked toward the cash register. "I haven't opened them, but I did push on the buttons, and they aren't spongy. These are new machines. When they came to set one up for the shipper side, they upgraded the one in here to match it."

"With the new machine design, you are less likely to have someone try the overlay skimmer." Conrad opened the machine and closed it. "It won't take long for the thieves to catch up with that though."

Arlene looked at Peggy and back at the chief. "Overlay skimmer?"

Conrad nodded. "That's when they place a replica over the top of the machine, and you don't even notice. It's quick and easy to do. The only actual difference is how the keys feel when you push them, but store owners don't really have a reason to push the keys on their own units."

"That's brilliant!" Arlene scowled, disappointed that she had to give thieves credit.

"It's gotten much more advanced since those. There are several methods now. Some even have Wi-Fi built in, and they have your card information transmitted to them before you can get back in your car!"

Arlene covered her mouth with her hand.

"The ones they have found recently in Paxton have been internal, so someone is popping off the top and connecting the skimmer inside. That's what we're looking for." Conrad walked around Peggy to go to the shipping side and grabbed the credit card machine on the counter.

"You're right. I need to start using cash," Arlene whispered to Peggy as she followed Conrad.

"Here we go." Conrad turned around to show the inside of the machine to Peggy. "Do you see this?" Conrad used the pencil on the counter to lift a wire up from the tangled mess of computer parts. It was a small plastic computer ribbon cord with a tiny green board on one end the size of a postage stamp.

"Yes."

Conrad waited when he heard Arlene's footsteps approaching.

"Can I see?" Arlene peeked over Peggy's left shoulder. "It looks like computer innards to me."

Peggy chuckled. "Me, too."

"Well, this is an internal skimmer." Conrad pulled out his handkerchief to unplug the ribbon cord from the machine and dropped it into a plastic bag he pulled from his pocket while he put their credit card reader back together.

Arlene gasped.

"How did this happen?" Peggy's mouth hung open. "These are barely a week old!"

Conrad looked around the ceiling. "Do you have cameras in here?"

Peggy moaned. "No, but they are on my to-do list."

Conrad chuckled. "You might want to bump them

up a little higher on the list."

"Oh my gosh! We need to warn people. We can print a report from the cash register or that software, can't we? I can send out an email and tell them to check their online statements. They can freeze those cards nowadays, right?" Arlene's hands were waving around with as much fluster as her words. "We need to do something."

When the phone rang in the craft shop, Arlene ran back to the cash wrap to answer it, and Conrad took the skimmer from Peggy.

"This may seem like a strange question, but have the store painters been in here? The guys that are painting the exteriors on all the businesses."

Peggy straightened. "Yeah. The one that seems to be the head guy, the older one, he shipped a package."

"Did he pay with a credit card?" Conrad opened his folder and dropped the skimmer inside.

"No, he paid cash."

Conrad nodded and turned to walk out the Salty Shipper's front door.

"Wait! Do you think he had something to do with this?"

"I don't know but I'm going to talk to him. Let me know if your customers find any fraudulent charges and send them my way, so I can take a report. Maybe we've found it quickly enough that they can get ahead of it. See you later."

"Okay, Chief." Peggy watched the front door close, wondering who had the opportunity to do this. It was time to make another list! She was turning into Cora Mae.

Chapter 24

Walking back to the police station, Conrad looked around Fennel Street for unfinished work. The painters would slip through his fingers if he didn't grab them before they were done. The only building on the main street that hadn't been painted was the old Hart & Grace Tax Service building.

His first instinct was to call Cora Mae. She knew a lot more about this mystery benefactor and their out-of-town painters than she was admitting. From the guilty glances he had watched her exchange with Jason Marks, he was in on it, too. He could call Georgia and put her on the task, but he decided using his own employee to exploit secrets from her son, the mayor's partner in crime, should probably be a last resort.

Maybe the painters went home on the weekend. Conrad stopped at the corner of Paprika Parkway and

Fennel Street to look both ways, then asked himself the obvious question he should have thought of when they first arrived in town. *Where are the painters staying?*

Conrad pushed through the side door of the Spicetown Police Department and waved at Officer Fred Rucker in dispatch to let him know he had returned, before ducking into his office.

Flipping through his phone, he tapped the number for the Nutmeg Inn and Levi Nachtmann answered on the first ring.

"Hey, Levi. It's Conrad Harris."

"Chief! How can I help you?"

"I was calling to see if the painters are staying with you. You know, those guys doing the storefronts downtown. I think there's only two of them, but there may be more. Are they staying with you."

Levi huffed. "They were for a minute. They came here when they first got to town, but they wanted secure storage for their equipment, and I don't have anything like that. They made a few phone calls and waited in the lobby for half an hour until someone called them back. The two of them left and we never heard from them again. I guess whoever they called found them another place."

"Did they have a reservation with you?"

"No, just walked in. They didn't say they were here to paint our buildings. They just said they had work tools and equipment that needed to be secured at night and asked for outside storage."

"Any idea who they called or where they might have gone?"

"No idea. I saw them on Fennel Street working one morning when I was walking over to the bakery. I asked them if they had found a good place to stay and they looked at me like they'd never seen me before. One of them finally said, 'yeah' and then climbed up a ladder, so I just kept walking. They are not the most personable pair."

"So, you don't have a name or address for them? They might go home over the weekend if they live nearby."

"We didn't get that far. Sorry. What are you wanting with those two?"

"Ah, I just had a few questions. I guess they can wait until Monday. Have a good weekend, Levi and tell Gretchen hello for me."

"You too, Chief. Thanks."

Conrad rolled his chair back from his desk. There was only one other place to stay in Spicetown and that was booked well in advance. The Keslar Mansion only offered a few rooms to the public as part of a travel promotion for the Irenic Wellness Spa. The painters must be staying in Paxton.

Conrad strolled down the hallway to dispatch to see

who was in the building. Gwen Kimball had been on day shift this month but was off today. Wink was trying out a new monthly rotation schedule and Conrad never knew where anyone was anymore. Officer Briscoe opened one eye as he approached but went back to sleep when he determined he was not Conrad's target.

"Asher!" Conrad found Roy Asher alone at an interview desk, hunched over a carbon pack form printing information in boxes with obvious force.

"Yeah, Chief?"

"What are you doing?"

"Fillin' out an evidence report." Roy lifted the top white copy to see if his information was clear on the pink copy below.

"You're supposed to do those on your laptop. They're all electronic now."

"Mine's not working, Chief. I can't get it to move from one box to another. I need to get Tabor to look at it." Officer Eugene Tabor was the unofficial technical support for the SPD.

"Did you try hitting the TAB button?" Conrad was not a computer wizard by any means, but he could build on what he learned. Asher seemed only able to take two steps back with each lesson. "Now someone else has to type this into the system."

Asher shrugged. "I figured Georgia would do it. Isn't that kinda part of her job?"

"It is not!" Conrad roared. Georgia Marks was a police officer assigned to dispatcher duties during the week, but she was Asher's equal. "But filling out forms on your laptop is very much a part of your job, so figure it out." Conrad spun around on his heel to walk down the hall and calm his frustration only to realize he had forgotten the whole reason he walked out there.

Returning to the front, Asher was still wrestling with paper and looked up in alarm at Conrad's return. "Sorry, Chief. I'm going to type it in. I just wanted to get it written down, so I don't forget it."

Conrad ignored Asher's comment. "Do you know about the painters that have been working downtown? They're repainting the storefronts on Fennel Street and a few others in the next block."

"Yeah! They look really nice, Chief."

The extra patience that Conrad needed to work with Roy Asher seemed to have taken the weekend off. "Do you know anything about these painters? Their names? Where they're from? Where they're staying?"

"Uh, I think they're staying at the mansion and their truck has Pennsylvania plates on it."

Startled at Asher's useful retort, Conrad took a deep relaxing breath. "Have you talked to them?"

"A little, kinda, you know just a hey-howdy. Nothing big."

Conrad waved his hands toward his chest to coax

out useful details from Asher and encourage him to explain so he didn't yell at him.

"They go out to the Wasabi Women's Club at night." Asher's gaze fell. He was always criticized for driving out there because it was outside the city limits. He only did it to turn around when he was on patrol, but everyone teased him because there were dancing girls out there.

"Were they involved in an altercation?" Spicetown responded to fights at the Wasabi when the county deputy sheriffs needed assistance or couldn't respond quickly.

"Nah, I just saw them walking out one night to their truck. I stopped to ask them where they were headed because the truck had out-of-state plates on it. I wanted to make sure they seemed okay to drive."

"Were they cordial?"

"Yeah. They said they were painting the storefronts and staying out at the old lady's mansion. I was a little concerned since the Keslar Mansion is clear on the other side of town, so I chatted him up a while to make sure he was steady on his feet before I left."

Conrad wondered if it was the alcohol or the uniform that made the painters respond politely. It could also be that Roy's expectations were lower. "Thanks."

"Glad I could help, Chief," Asher shouted as Conrad walked down the hallway to his office.

Conrad had the phone number for the Keslar Mansion memorized. When Grace Keslar first opened her home to visitors of her spa, he had been called to make frequent visits out there to manage misguided guests with ulterior motives.

"Good afternoon, Chief!" Grace Keslar had a smile in her voice.

"Good afternoon, Mrs. Keslar. I'm sorry to bother you, but I was wondering whether the painters that were working downtown might be staying with you. One of my officers said he thought they were guests of yours."

"Oh, yes! I rarely see them. They are staying in some extra rooms on the south side of the house because we were already booked with our spa guests. It is just a place to stay for them through the work week. They are not dining with my guests."

"I didn't realize you rented rooms out like that without reservations. I thought you were strictly using the travel packages for the spa." It was possible that the painters had called the mansion from the Nutmeg Inn lobby, but it didn't seem likely someone new to town would think to do that.

"Not usually. You're correct. Just when there is a special need."

Conrad hummed. "So, how did you find out they had a special need?"

"Ah, I got a call that they were here to paint downtown but needed somewhere to stay that had a storage area. They have a lot of gadgets in their truck that they use but no way to secure them at night."

"I see. Did they call you?"

"No. No, it was Jason Marks. I think the boy is trying to help them get settled in."

"Ah, yes. Thank you, Mrs. Keslar, and you have a pleasant day."

"Thank you, Chief. You, too!"

Chapter 25

"What do we do now?" Arlene sat down on the sofa when she had a break between customers. "Do you have to file a report?"

Peggy was sitting in the chair with her notebook in her lap. "I don't think so. The chief didn't say I needed to go down to the police department, but maybe I should."

"What are you working on?"

"I'm trying to figure out who had the opportunity to put that skimmer in there. I know we don't cover the shipping side every minute of the day, but we do usually run over there when we hear the bell."

Arlene jumped up. "I'm going to go print a list of customers we've had. We need to try to contact them. I'll be right back."

"Good idea." Peggy started her list backwards. Darryl Figgins had been over there alone this morning to hang the door. There was Cecil Ryman from Volker Electric, who put up the monitor.

Arlene returned with a receipt tape in her hand. "You know this could have happened on opening day. It was crazy in there that morning, and I know I wasn't paying attention to the counter at all."

"I was there though. I'm thinking it's more likely to have happened when someone had to wait on us to get there or they were there working. You know we've had several workers over there."

"Fig from this morning." Arlene held up a finger. "Was Cecil over there alone when he was here?"

"Yes, a couple of times."

"But he brought another boy with him one day. It was Ricky, the boy that does the sound system at the community center when they have a play."

"Ricky Deavers." Peggy added the name to her list. "Rumor has it that he has been in jail a few times."

"For stealing?" Arlene's eyes grew wide in concern.

"I think it was drugs."

"Oh." Arlene frowned, uncertain if that was better. "People who use drugs steal to finance their drug problem."

Peggy smiled. "That's what I've heard, too. They could do it together, Cecil and Ricky. I think they are friends, and they may work as a team. One distracts the owner and the other plants the skimmer."

"Was Andy over on the other side alone?"

"He was, but I don't think Andy would do something like that. Maybe it was a customer." Peggy chewed her bottom lip and tried to remember each customer. "Can you remember anyone coming in the shipping side while you were busy over here? Maybe when I stepped out to pick up lunches? I had that happen the other day with the painter. The day you went to the doctor he came in for shipping and I had him wait a few minutes because I was checking Annie Walker out. It was less than five minutes though."

"I don't think I've had anyone over there waiting alone when you've been gone, but it only takes one minute if you know what you're doing. The chief had that thing apart in a second."

"True." Peggy added Joe the painter to her list and tapped the pen against her notebook.

Cecil Ryman
Ricky Deavers
Darryl Figgins
Andy Gentry
Joe the Painter

"You might want to look through this list of customers." Arlene handed Peggy the report she printed. "Maybe it will remind you of something. Did you ever go back in the storeroom looking for a box and leave someone up there?"

"I haven't. As far as I remember, these are the only people that have had the opportunity to plant that thing, other than you and me." Peggy showed Arlene her list. "I guess I need to take this to the chief."

"You aren't going to put me on that list, are you?" Arlene inhaled until her chest expanded.

Peggy chuckled. "Of course not. I'm a bigger suspect than you!"

"Why do you say that?"

"You already told the chief that checking the machines was my department!" Peggy pointed at herself and laughed.

Arlene squinted with a sly smile and a sinister nod. "Yeah, that was all part of my plan."

Peggy laughed and reached into her pocket for her cell phone. "I think I'll send the chief a text message with these names. He zeroed in on the painter first, but I'm not sure why."

Peggy tapped away on her phone. Having his cell phone number had been a big help these last few months. Playing phone tag with the police station could be frustrating. She just hoped he didn't mind that she continued to use it.

Just when Conrad had exhausted his attempts to locate the painters and was resigning himself to waiting for Monday morning, he received Peggy's text message. He had arrested Ricky Deavers before and knew the other names well. Darryl Figgins did not live in Spicetown and wouldn't be back at the Keslar Mansion until Monday. Andy Gentry was an unlikely suspect, but he would give him a call.

"Asher!" Conrad roared.

After several seconds, Roy Asher appeared at Conrad's door. "Yeah, Chief. Did you call me?"

Conrad held out a piece of paper. "I need you to pick these two up and bring them in for questioning. They both work at Volker Electric, but I don't know if they're working today."

"Yeah. Yeah, Chief. I know 'em. I can do that. I'll get right on it."

As Roy turned to leave, Conrad stopped him. "And Roy?"

"Yeah, Chief?"

"Don't arrest them. It's just questioning. They might be witnesses. I just need to ask them a few questions. Don't spook 'em." Asher could amplify the importance of simple tasks and don the persona of a sheriff in the wild west if he was let loose without direction.

"Gotcha, Chief." Roy rushed down the hallway and

out the front door glancing at the parking lot camera before jumping into his squad car.

Conrad felt guilty after every impatient interaction with Roy, but some days he just didn't have it in him to coddle him. Asher's wide-eyed nervous reaction always made him feel like he was the bad guy.

Harold "Wink" Hobson walked in the side door of the police department and slowly passed Conrad's office door with a sly smile.

"Wink!" Conrad barked and held his hand out to stop him. He wasn't sure why he was arriving for night shift so early, but he didn't get the opportunity to talk to him often.

"Hey, Chief. What's up?"

"I'd just like to take this opportunity to go on record and tell you that I really hate this schedule rotation thing you've started."

Wink clutched his stomach when he laughed. "Noted, but I'm sure you can admit that you understand why I did it." His official reasoning was to give every officer an opportunity to learn and become comfortable with office day shift and night patrols.

"Oh, yeah. I knew that from the start, but I didn't know how miserable it would make me."

"Only twenty-seven more days left and then we'll rotate again." Wink tried to swallow his laughter knowing Conrad could rewrite that schedule any time he wanted.

"Why didn't you put Georgia in the rotation? Let Asher sit in dispatch for a few weeks. It might be good for him."

Wink lifted an eyebrow as if he was considering it. He knew Asher had a tendency to disrespect Georgia's contribution and the experience might offer some growth. "We could."

"I'll see how it goes, but I may just swap them since they are both on days. Georgia hasn't been out on the road for a long time. I'll talk to her about it."

"Let me know how it goes."

Conrad nodded as Wink headed down the hallway. Reaching for the radio, he turned up the volume so he could follow Asher's activity and try to be patient.

Calling Andy Gentry was going to be touchy. He had forgotten who Andy's mother was, and although the boy was no trouble, his mother sent Conrad running in the other direction every time. With fingers crossed he dialed the number, hoping Andy's stepfather Rodney Maddox would answer instead, but this had not been a lucky day for him.

"Hello."

"Mrs. Maddox? This is Police Chief Conrad Harris. Is your son, Andy, at home?" Conrad could tell by the sound of Carmen Maddox's voice that she was agitated by something before she even said hello. Carmen was always hot or cold, never in the normal range, and both extremes made Conrad jumpy.

"What's this about, Chief?"

"Is Andy at home right now? I just need to speak to him. It'll only take a few minutes."

"Andy's not home, but I'm not letting you talk to him unless you tell me what's going on."

Conrad knew Andy was over eighteen and the argument wasn't worth having. "I'll contact him later. Thank you." Conrad hung up without waiting for her response. He would have to go through Rodney on Monday and then run Andy down.

When his phone chimed with a new text message, he held his breath hoping it was not Roy Asher.

Sorry to bug you again, but Slim Pickens keeps coming up in conversation. Is it okay if I check with Slim and see who he's had working out there since November?

Conrad frowned at Peggy's text message and agreed it was a business name that showed up more than once, but Peggy just had a skimmer in her own store. How could an employee of Slim Pickens' plant it at the Carom Seed?

Conrad had time to kill waiting on Asher, so he

decided it couldn't hurt. He hadn't talked to Melvin Pickens in a long time either. He'd return Peggy's text message later.

Chapter 26

Arlene finished helping a customer with a shipment and returned to the craft side of the store. Sully was walking around the new display she had set up that morning by the entrance, sniffing and studying it to see if it passed inspection. Looking out the front windows, she could see the flurry of activity on Fennel Street had died away.

"It's about time to close. Did you hear back from the chief? What did he say?"

Peggy closed her sewing kit and carried the wedding dress skirt to the sewing machine. "He didn't answer. He must be busy."

"What are you going to do?"

"I thought about just driving out to Slim Pickens. I haven't seen them in a long time. I could buy something and act like I was just passing by." Peggy arranged the dress carefully on the sewing table so she would be able to resume the alterations on Monday.

"But they probably aren't there this late. You'd drive all the way out there and some stranger would be at the counter."

Peggy nodded. "You're right. I should just wait. The chief has already told me to stop getting involved. I don't want to get in trouble with him again." Peggy had promised him she wouldn't go off doing crazy things without talking to him first, and she had been careful the last few months to not break that promise.

"He may have already talked to Melvin Pickens. He knows what he's doing, so I wouldn't worry if I were you. If he doesn't answer you this weekend, you can ask him again Monday." Arlene picked up one of Sully's toys and tossed it into his crate before glancing at the clock. It was still too early to close up, but Arlene was afraid if she sat down, it would be more difficult to get back up.

The bells on the door jingled and Sully's stubby tail began to dance when Valerie Duffy slipped in, her forehead creased in apology. "Sorry, guys. I know you are getting ready to close. Hello, Mr. Sully!" Valerie scratched Sully's head as he panted. "I just wanted to drop off this swatch."

Peggy walked over and took the small piece of cloth Valerie offered and rubbed her fingers over it. "This is chiffon."

"Oh," Valerie shrugged. "I don't know my fabrics,

but this is the sample from the bridesmaid dresses. My dress inserts don't have to match exactly, but I just wanted you to see them. I'd probably rather mine be a little paler in color, but as long as it doesn't clash, it will be fine."

"I've ordered it, but I haven't gotten a shipping notice yet. Let me show you what I ordered." Peggy went to the storeroom and came back with her laptop.

"Are you getting excited?" Arlene scrunched her shoulders up around her ears and smiled.

"I am. I'm getting a little stressed out that I am not organized enough and I'm going to overlook something important. It's not just the wedding. We have the land sale, the utilities, and the mobile home stuff to work through. After that, we have to do something about furniture!" Valerie threw her hands out. "It's a lot!"

"Oh, but that's the fun part. It is a lot of work, but it's all effort going toward making your perfect day and the happily ever after. You'll look back later when you're rested and realize this was the best time of your life!" Arlene still remembered every minute of her wedding day, the good and the bad.

"My mom is sure having fun. She's exhausting me with details." Valerie laughed.

Peggy turned her laptop around and pointed. "That's what I ordered. If that's too deep, I can look around for something lighter."

"It should be okay. There will be netting and stuff over it, right?"

"Tulle. Yes, it will be underneath the tulle."

Valerie stared at the photo trying to picture her finished dress in her mind. "Maybe a sash in the peach? I think I'd like that if the color is close to what the girls are wearing."

"Sure! That's easy to do. We can decide how wide or how long once I get the pieces back together." Peggy waved her hand over the sewing machine table where Angela's wedding dress was in several pieces.

"That sounds good!" Valerie leaned down and scratched Sully behind the ears. "I need to meet Derek down at Juniper Junction at five o'clock and I'm sure you are ready to close for the day, but I'm glad I caught you before you left."

"A Saturday night dinner date!" Arlene smiled. "That's nice."

"It's really a strategy meeting so we can go over our list of things to do." Valerie chuckled. "We were supposed to go look at mobile homes today, but he got called in to cover someone's shift, which happens all the time. They pull him from one store to the other to fill in for people who call out sick or don't show up at all. It's impossible to make plans with him."

Arlene patted Valerie on the back as she walked toward the door. "Pretty soon he'll be saying that about you and all of your pet emergencies."

Valerie nodded as she pulled the door open. "You're probably right."

"I'll text you when the fabric arrives." Peggy waved as Valerie slipped out the door.

Conrad glanced at the security monitor when he saw Officer Asher's squad car pull in to park. It idled for several minutes until Roy stepped out of the car alone. Conrad shook his head and reached for the weekly shift schedule to see who was assigned day shift on Monday. When he saw Roy Asher was listed as the day officer, he picked up his mobile phone and called Georgia Marks.

"Hello."

"Hey, Georgia. It's Conrad. Sorry to bother you on a Saturday."

"It's no bother, Chief. What can I do for you?"

"How do you feel about working the street again? Taking a rotation as day officer?"

Several seconds of silence preceded Georgia's response. "Well, it's been a long time..."

"Wink has everyone doing monthly rotations and I thought you might like to be included. It wouldn't hurt the other staff to take a turn at dispatch either. They need to be more comfortable there in case they're needed, too. Do you have any objections?" Conrad could force the issue. Georgia was a trained and experienced police officer just like the others, but she had volunteered for the dispatcher role when no one else wanted it, and she was good at it.

"Okay, Chief. Yeah, let's give it a try. I might be a little rusty, but you're right. I want to see if I can still do it."

"Thanks. See you Monday." Conrad hung up his phone and saw Roy Asher hovering in his doorway. "Come on in. What happened?"

"Nothing, Chief. I just couldn't find them. Ricky's mom said he went to Pine Lake fishing with his dad. He'll be around tomorrow maybe."

"And Cecil?"

"No clue." Asher shook his head in bewilderment. "He wasn't home or at work."

Conrad wasn't surprised. "Did you try calling them? I know we have Ricky's number and Volker Electric probably has a phone number for both of them."

Asher inhaled and his eyes swam around the room searching for a response.

"Never mind. I'll take care of it later. There's been a change in the shift schedule. You'll still be on days starting Monday, but you'll be on the dispatch desk."

"Dispatch! Holy cow, Chief. Why do I gotta do that? Is Georgie sick?"

"No, but she could be. Everyone needs to be cross trained. We need all officers to be able to fill in wherever they're needed. We're a small department and we can't be specialized."

"Why you gotta start with me? What did I do?"

"I just told you why." Asher's whining was raising Conrad's blood pressure. "And you're about to talk yourself into a permanent reassignment."

"Sorry, Chief. I'll do my best." Asher slipped quietly away and down the hall.

Conrad pushed back from his desk. He should just go home and try to salvage some of the weekend. He wouldn't find the painter until Monday and that's who he really wanted to talk to. Maybe he could take Briscoe for a walk down by the lake. It might improve his mood and keep his mind off food, then he remembered Peggy's text.

He texted her back, telling her that he would request an employee list, and then reached for his desk phone. He didn't need Peggy going down there and stirring things up. After a quick internet search, he dialed the Slim Pickens' convenience store.

"Pickens." A gravelly voice barked impatiently into the phone.

"Melvin?" Conrad said cautiously.

"Yeah!" The voice lit up with recognition.

"This is Chief Harris."

"Hey! Howdy, Chief. How're you doin' these days?"

Conrad chuckled. Melvin Pickens was probably not as old as he looked, but the passage of time never dampened his enthusiasm for life. "I'm pretty good. I've got a favor to ask of you. Nothing urgent, but I do need some information when you get a chance."

"Sure! I'm an open book. What can I do you for?"

"I'm investigating some credit card fraud and I know you had a bit of that back in the winter."

"Yep, I did, and I about threw them machines in the trash. What good is all this advance technology if all it does is teach people new ways to steal?"

"I hear you, but it's kicked up again. It's happening in Paxton and we're seeing a little bit spill over into Spicetown, so I'm trying to nip this in the bud."

"I check mine all the time, just like you showed me."

"That's good to hear. I was wondering if you could send me a list of all the employees you've had over the last year. I can run out and pick it up from you if that's easier."

Melvin hummed. "I think Edie can put that together for you and do you an email so you don't have to make a trip. There's been a lot of 'em. These kids don't stick around long."

"It might be that one of those kids is now working somewhere that's being skimmed and it might give us a good lead. It's a long shot, but worth a phone call."

"Sure thing, Chief. We'll get that to ya!"

"Thanks, Melvin, and tell Edie hello for me, too."

Conrad logged out of his computer, feeling a small sense of calm returning until Wink Hobson's head popped around the corner of the door.

"You leaving?"

"Yes, I've had enough fun today." Conrad took a calming breath before rising from his chair.

Wink chuckled. "You got Asher boo-hooing in the break room. He thinks he's being punished for something."

"Could it be because I caught him handwriting his reports? Or maybe it was his assumption that it was the dispatcher's job to type his reports into the system. Or it could be because I sent him to find two kids and he didn't even think to try a phone first. And all of those things happened just today." Conrad tapped his finger hard on his desktop.

Wink grinned. "Yep, it could be, but that's every day with Asher."

Conrad huffed and pushed his chair under his desk. "I just wasn't up to it today."

"Could it be because it's a Saturday and it should be your day off? Or maybe because you didn't think to call the two kids yourself first. Or it could be because the Spicetown Chief of Police needs to go get a donut!" Wink laughed alone, but he saw Conrad's demeanor change and knew he would accept some of the blame for his impatience.

"It could be." Conrad said as Wink was walking away. He had been short with everyone this week and he needed to find a way to diet that didn't alienate everyone around him.

Conrad waved at Officer Fred Rucker, who was sitting in the dispatcher's cubicle, as he walked out the side door of the station. Fred was the only person that hadn't gotten on his last nerve today, but that might be because he didn't even talk to him.

Chapter 27

Monday morning, Cora Mae left the office on foot early to drop off Jason's article at the Spicetown Star before picking up a cake at the bakery for a City Hall employee party. Everyone in the front office had contributed something for the luncheon. She had planned to bake a cake over the weekend and had completely forgotten all about it. She knew Vicki would have something made up to save her.

As she turned the corner from Fennel Street to Clove Street, she saw Conrad peeking through the windows of the abandoned tax office with both hands cupped around his eyes to block out the sun's glare. He stepped back and waited for her to approach when he saw her.

"You're out and about early."

"Just headed to the Star. Is something going on

inside?" Cora glanced in the window.

"No, I'm just waiting to see if the painters show up. I need to talk to them." Conrad put his hands in his pants pockets and tried to look casual.

"Whatever for?"

"Aren't they supposed to paint this building next?"

"I don't know. I'm not even sure they plan to paint this unless Jeremiah gives them approval to do it. I haven't been down the other streets to see what they've finished."

"Who keeps track of them? Jason? Would he know where they plan to be next?"

Cora Mae scowled and waited for Conrad to answer her original question.

"What?" Conrad held his hands out. "I just need to ask them a few questions, that's all. They have been on the street for weeks now and they may have seen something that would help me with my fraud case."

Cora Mae smirked and rolled her eyes. She knew when Conrad was speaking nonsense. "Come on, Connie. You can do better than that. What are you up to?"

"I'm not up to anything! One of the painters was at the site where I found a skimmer. I want to know who else he saw."

"You want to question him. These guys are here providing a free service to this town, and I don't want you bullying them." Cora Mae straightened her shoulders as her eyebrows clinched together.

"That doesn't mean they can steal from us." Conrad glanced over at the Caraway Cafe, but they were not open yet.

"Pfft." Cora walked around Conrad and continued towards the newspaper office on Tarragon Street without looking back. The topic was not worth an argument because she knew the painters were not planning to come back to town until Friday.

Conrad crossed Fennel Street before he had to walk by the Fennel Street Bakery. The cinnamon roll aroma was like a punch in the stomach, but he was trying to resist. He could see Peggy moving around inside the Carom Seed Craft Corner and he knocked on her window.

"Good morning." Peggy held the door open and flipped on the lights. She had just arrived, and Sully was still wandering around inside the store. "Come on inside."

"I just wanted to let you know I talked to Melvin Pickens."

Arlene walked in the front door and Conrad stepped to the side as everyone said good morning.

"Was he able to tell you who worked there?"

Arlene put her purse under the counter and busied

herself at the register so she could listen in.

"Yes, he sent me a list. The names mean nothing to me, but I don't have employee lists from all the other shop owners to compare it to. I could request that, I guess, but he's had quite a few."

"Can I see it?" Peggy reached her hand out and Conrad handed it to her.

Peggy studied the list and looked at Arlene, but her eyes were blank as she searched her memory.

"What do you see?" Conrad stepped forward seeing wheels turn in Peggy's mind.

"Arlene, do you remember the day that Cecil and Ricky both came over to try to fix that monitor?" Peggy pointed toward the Salty Shipper.

"Yeah."

"In the middle of all that, Valerie stopped by to introduce Derek. Right?"

"Yes. You were over there talking to Cecil, and Ricky had just arrived. I took them over to that side to see you."

"But then Valerie wanted to talk to us. Remember? She wanted to show us a picture and we came back over here to look at her phone."

"That's right. Derek seemed to know Cecil and he stayed over there with them." Arlene nodded, but she didn't know why they were rehashing the day.

Peggy glared at Arlene. "Derek is on this list. Was

he over there by himself at any time?"

Arlene bit her bottom lip. "No, I don't think so. I don't remember when Cecil and Ricky left though."

"But Cecil and Ricky were busy working. They would have had their back to Derek. They were mounting a new monitor at the back door. They might have been talking, but they weren't looking at him. I should have known this days ago!" Peggy slapped her leg. "Valerie told me she met Derek when he worked for Slim Pickens last summer and her father had his credit card scammed from Slim Pickens right before Christmas. The list says Derek worked there until February. Darryl Figgins had his card number stolen at Slim Pickens in February."

"Now, wait." Conrad waved his hand to settle the tension. Peggy was running away with herself again. "We don't know anything yet."

"Derek would know how to pop those covers off. He's a retail manager in Paxton and works for a company that owns a bunch of convenience stores. I bet he checks those machines himself so he can open and shut them without any suspicion. He can plant those things and remove them anytime he wants, even on camera!"

Arlene's bottom lip pushed out as wrinkles formed across her forehead. She didn't want any of this to be true. "I did wonder how a gas station manager could buy land and a mobile home."

"Huh? Slow down, ladies. You're losing me. How do you know Derek Fields?"

"He's engaged to Valerie Duffy. Come sit down, Chief." Peggy motioned Conrad to the back of the store. "Would you like some coffee? I haven't made any yet, but I need some."

Conrad shook his head.

"I'll put a pot on." Arlene rushed to the storeroom, almost tripping over Sully who stood at his crate door ready for his morning nap.

Conrad listened for almost an hour, taking notes as Peggy and Arlene powered through the story from the beginning. It was clear he still needed to do some legwork, but they had given him a solid suspect. It was possible that one of the stores Derek worked for now would also show up on the credit card lists he had collected from recent victims. If this panned out, it could strengthen his relationship with the new sheriff, as well.

"Okay, I got it." Conrad stood up and yanked on his belt for more breathing room. "Let me get busy. If Derek or the girl come in here for some reason, text me. Otherwise, mums the word." Conrad mimicked zipping his lips and looked at both Peggy and Arlene. "I'll be in touch."

Conrad didn't even pause to revel in the bakery smells. He hurried down the street to get back to the office. Georgia had been giving Roy a refresher on how to work the radio when he left, and he hoped that lesson didn't last all month. It was time for them both to start the day with new assignments. He worked on the interview questions he would ask as he walked.

Barreling down the hallway of the PD, Georgia and Roy both looked up in surprise and Conrad waited a few seconds to calm his breathing. He might have walked faster than usual, and he felt a little overheated.

"Georgia, I need you to get in touch with Cecil Ryman and Ricky Deavers. They both work for Volker Electric. See if you can get them in here for questioning. They aren't being arrested. I just need to talk to them."

"Okay, Chief." Georgia was seated at the day officer's desk and fumbled for a moment to get acclimated to the computer there but went to a search page to get a phone number.

"Asher, I need you to pull me a sheet on a Derek Fields. He lives in Paxton, about 27 years old, and works for some company that runs a bunch of convenience stores over there. I need to know if he has a history and I need contact information for his employer."

"It's probably Kamal Kart Inc. They own a dozen of those places in Paxton." Asher spun his chair toward the computer and his fingers hesitated over the keyboard while he searched his memory for the steps he needed to take.

Conrad stood there waiting to see if the hamster on

the wheel in Roy's head would be able to get things moving without Georgia pointing it all out again, but he did. Conrad went to the office and grabbed his pitcher to fetch water for his coffee maker and work on his interview questions. As he walked into the break room, he stopped and looked around.

There were red and white tablecloths spread over two tables, with plastic trays and bowls filled with carrot sticks, cauliflower, broccoli, and cucumbers with slices of cheese on the side. A platter was heaped with bananas and grapes with apple slices in a covered bowl and two cans of assorted nuts.

Conrad didn't move, but yelled out, "What's going on in here?"

"Help yourself, Chief." Georgia hollered back and then quickly dialed the phone number to Volker Electric.

Conrad strolled back to the lobby with his water pitcher still in his hand. Seeing Georgia on the phone, he looked at Asher and hooked his thumb over his shoulder. "What's all that about?"

Asher shrugged with his mouth hanging open in innocence. "Georgia brought it in. She said we needed some healthy snacks. I guess she's on a health kick or something."

Conrad smirked. He knew Wink was behind this. He returned to the break room, filled his pitcher with water and filled a plate with fruit and nuts before returning to his office to call the sheriff. It wasn't a donut, but it was something.

Chapter 28

After a long day, Conrad felt he had handed the sheriff's department a strong case. The county had arrested Derek at work in Paxton and compared his prints to those found on the skimmer they had discovered a few days ago at a station owned by Kamal Kart Inc.

Ricky and Cecil had both provided statements that they saw Derek pull the cover off the credit card machine, but they thought Derek was just playing around with it at the time. Once the credit card statements were collected, Conrad saw that every victim had gotten gas at a Kamal Kart owned station in Paxton within the last two months.

Derek didn't confess, but he did hire an attorney, and the prosecutors were confident they had what they needed to convict him. Conrad's work was done.

After calling Peggy to give her an update, which he

did not permit her to share, he called Cora Mae.

"Hello, Connie."

The greeting was normal, but the tone was frosty. He knew he would have to mend fences. "Do you have dinner plans? I thought you might like to go to Old Thyme Italian."

"Do you have a riddle to solve and need a pizza?" It was an inside joke between them.

Conrad heard a small smile in those words, a small opportunity to turn things around. "Nope, case solved. I think I need a ravioli celebration. I'm hungry!"

Cora Mae giggled. "Case solved, huh? You found the credit card skimmer thief?"

"Well, I didn't solve it. Peggy did, but that's classified information."

Cora Mae chuckled. "So, who was it?"

"Derek Fields. He's not from Spicetown, so you may not know him. He was engaged to Valerie Duffy, Angela and David's daughter. You know them."

"Oh, my! Yes, I do. That's terrible. I feel so bad for her."

"At least she found out before she married him!"

Cora sighed. "That's true. That's a blessing."

"So, are you hungry?"

"If you go eat ravioli, you'll undo all the hard work you've done this week." Cora knew the battles of dieting. She had struggled with it for the last twenty years. It was hard.

"I didn't eat lunch today. Georgia fed me grass and weeds instead. I deserve a decent meal."

"Okay, on one condition."

Conrad moaned. He never fared well in these deals. "What condition?"

"That you let me give you some suggestions on this diet. Let me help. I know I don't set a good example, but you never saw an extra pound on George Bingham, did you? I've had a lot of experience and I think I know what will work best for you. I think you can lose weight without feeling hungry."

Conrad hummed. Over the phone, she couldn't see the doubt on his face, but the silence conveyed it.

"It doesn't work on me because I don't eat from hunger, but you do. There is a way to eat satisfying meals and lose weight."

"Do I get pizza and donuts?" Conrad smiled, waiting for her to scold him.

"Oh, Connie." Cora Mae huffed in defeat.

"We can discuss all this over ravioli. I'll meet you there at six."

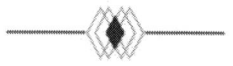

Although weeks of awkward silence passed, Peggy continued to work on Valerie's dress. No one reached out to her, but it was always possible Derek could be exonerated. Peggy had to be ready in case Valerie wanted to move forward. By the time Arlene heard through the grapevine that the engagement had been broken, Peggy had already reassembled Angela's wedding dress with the promised adjustments and Peggy knew she had to call her.

"I'm so nervous." Arlene fanned herself with a Leisure Arts afghan pattern booklet.

The dress looked beautiful on her standing dress form, but no one had ever tried it on. She left it on the stand so Angela and David could see it before she put it away. She had asked them to come pick it up and they were due to arrive any moment.

"I hope she doesn't talk about Derek. She doesn't know you were involved, does she?"

"Me?" Peggy pointed at her chest in teasing. "You were there, too."

Arlene shook her head and smiled. "I plead the fifth."

"I don't think anyone outside Cora Mae and the chief know we had anything to do with his arrest and I think we need to keep it that way."

"Oh, I agree! I just hope this isn't weird."

"Me, too." Peggy was also concerned about

whether she was getting paid.

When the Duffys finally arrived, Peggy was on the shipping side finishing a shipment with a customer and she hurried to get back. She didn't want to leave Arlene with it. As she came through the pass-through, she saw Angela and David both standing at the dress form staring at the dress, as Angela stroked her fingers over the satin.

"Hi there." Peggy glanced at Arlene with a question in her eyes. Arlene seemed frozen in place. "Do you like it?" No one was talking. "I thought it turned out pretty well."

"Oh, Peggy." David glanced over his shoulder. "Yes, it's really beautiful. I'm sure Valerie will be pleased."

"It's gorgeous, Peg." Angela sighed. "It has a whole new life in it. I just hope someday Valerie gets to wear it."

"Oh, I'm sure she will!" Peggy rushed around behind the mannequin and grabbed the large white box. "Let me pack it up for you. I just left it on the form so you could see it."

"Oh, look at the time!" Angela looked at David. "I need to get to Chervil's. Can you take care of this and let me run down there? I'll meet you at the car."

"Sure, honey. Go ahead. I'll be there in a minute."

Peggy tensed. That seemed a little staged and she was afraid Angela was trying to avoid a discussion of payment for the work Peggy had done. Glancing at Arlene, she finally nodded her head at Angela as she said goodbye.

"Peggy, I wanted to talk to you a minute alone." David sat down on the sofa and Peggy felt her stomach clench, but she continued packing the dress into the box.

"Our thirtieth wedding anniversary is coming up in a few months and I'm planning to ask Angela if she'd like to have a renewal ceremony at the church."

Suddenly, Arlene came back to life. "Oh, David. That's a wonderful idea. I'm sure she'd love that!"

Peggy was not yet won over. She now feared he would ask for the dress to be reverted back to its original style and she was debating if she could just say no.

David put his finger across his lips. "It's a secret."

"Of course. Of course!" Arlene sat down in the chair beside the sofa. "Angela could wear the dress!" Peggy's eyes shot daggers at Arlene. "The new dress! This dress. It looked like she really loved it."

"That's what I'm hoping." David pulled out his wallet and handed Arlene his credit card as Peggy relaxed. "What I wanted to know is whether one of you could make one of those stitched plaques for me." David held his hands up in a rectangular shape. "I don't know what it's called, but you sew on material with colored thread and frame it."

"Embroidery or cross stitch." Peggy looked around

the room for a sample and pointed. "This is embroidery."

"Yeah, like that. Can you make me one of those? Can I give you the words and you can do that?"

"We can. When do you need it?" Peggy looked over David's head as Arlene returned with the credit card, nodding to her that it went through.

"Oh, not until our anniversary." David fished around in the flaps of his wallet and pulled out a small piece of paper to hand to Peggy. "It's just a part of my vows."

> *I'm so proud of what we created: Our beautiful child, a wonderful marriage and for what I've become because of you.*
> *Love, David*

"That shouldn't be a problem. We can add some flowers around it and frame it for you." Peggy handed the slip of paper to Arlene.

"Great!" David jumped up off the sofa. "Wait until I call you to confirm, though. You never know, she may not say yes."

Peggy smiled as she handed him the box. "I'll wait to hear from you. We can alter the dress if it doesn't fit. Just let us know."

"I will. Thank you, both. We appreciate everything you did." David rushed out the door with the large bulky box under his arm.

Arlene sighed as she sat down on the sofa. "Isn't that sweet? Isn't it nice to see something good come out of all this mess?"

Peggy hummed. "A fitting end."

Next in the Carom Seed Cozies:

Read the first chapter here~>

Chapter 1

Peggy's feet slapped the hot pavement of Paprika Parkway as Sully pulled her along by the leash. She had taken him out early for a morning walk today hoping to beat the heat, but when she had to change her usual walking route, it put her in the direct sun.

Approaching Fennel Street, she saw Mayor Bingham sitting on one of the new iron benches outside Chervil Drugs swinging her feet forward and back as she glanced over her shoulder.

"Good morning! Are you testing out the new bench?"

Startled, Cora Mae swiveled around in her seat and smiled. "Hi, Peggy! Yes, and this one is a little high for me." Cora's feet did not touch the ground. "I'm waiting on Ted to refill a prescription for me." Cora patted the seat next to her. "Give it a try!"

Sully greeted Cora Mae and then Peggy sat down

beside her. "I would be in the air conditioning, if I was you. It's already too warm for us." Sully's tongue hung out of the right side of his mouth dripping saliva on the sidewalk as he panted. "We usually walk around this block because it's shaded, but you can't get down Fennel Street again today. If they don't clean this mess up by tomorrow, Sully and I are going to skip the walk altogether."

"I know. It's gone on too long. The chief said he would check on things, but having a semi-trailer truck parked on Fennel Street for two days has not just been a headache, but I'm sure it's hurting everyone's business. Saucy told me he couldn't even walk by there to get to the bakery yesterday." Harvey "Saucy" Salzman liked his morning social at the Fennel Street Bakery every so often. He didn't go daily, but when the weather was nice, he liked to stop in for the camaraderie.

"I think everyone's business has been hurt. No one has anywhere to park. They drive down just to see what's going on, but when they can't park, they move on. I can't even see the bakery and I'm right across the street from it!"

"I'm surprised there hasn't been an accident. It's blocking the entire lane and you can't see around it." Cora Mae waved when she saw Chief Harris walking down the opposite side of the street with his dog, Briscoe, leading the way toward the new business.

"There goes the chief. Maybe he'll hurry them along."

Regina Adkins was opening a new dress shop in the storefront next to the Fennel Street Bakery called Sassafras. The semi-trailer truck had arrived yesterday to unload her merchandise and equipment. The sidewalk was littered with boxes and handcarts while several people walked in and out of the dress shop.

"Have you met the owner, Regina?" Peggy scratched the top of Sully's head. His breathing had slowed but he needed water.

"I haven't, but it seems everyone else has. She's been in City Hall, but I must have been out at the time. I was planning to stop in and introduce myself, but I didn't want to bother anyone while they were moving. Dorothy said she's been in the Caraway Cafe almost daily, but I always miss her. Is she nice?"

Peggy's forehead creased as she searched for the proper word to describe a slightly pretentious middle-aged city person having a mid-life crisis. "She's different."

Cora raised one eyebrow and smiled. "I understand she's brought a group of employees with her. I guess she doesn't plan to hire local people."

"My understanding is that this group travels with her to set things up. Sometimes she leaves one behind to manage the place and the group moves on with her. This time she said she plans to stay and give small town life a try, so I assume she'll hire local people once they open."

"Interesting business plan." Cora Mae smirked. "Dorothy tells me the team she brought is mostly young people. I think they've come in the cafe. I wonder where they're staying."

"Oh, Clyde's got them scattered all over town." Peggy chuckled. Clyde Newman worked for Red Pepper Realty and had rented the storefront to Regina. He had also been helping her look for a permanent home, but in the meantime, he found temporary rental accommodations for the girls. "Regina is in the Nutmeg Inn, but the others are in rentals around town."

"Well, I'm sure I'll eventually run into them all."

"We need to be getting back to the store. Arlene will be missing us and I think Sully needs to cool down." Sully got to his feet when Peggy stood.

"Okay, I'll check on Ted's progress. See you later."

Regina Adkins rushed down the sidewalk toward Conrad Harris as he approached. He saw Briscoe's tail and ears quiver with tension. "Whoa!" Conrad held his hand out to stop Regina and pulled Briscoe back to stand at his side. "You don't want to rush up on a police dog like that."

"Oh, sorry, Chief. I'll be careful." Regina calmed

her voice and stayed several feet away.

"How's it going with this?" Conrad waved his hand at the 18-wheeler blocking all access to the downtown community and the major east-west road through town.

"I know what you're going to say, Chief."

"You do?" Conrad's eyebrows rose and he tilted his head. "What am I going to say?"

Regina hesitated a moment. "You want to know when it's going to move."

"I know when it's going to move. You told me yesterday that it would be gone by noon today. Do you also know what I'm thinking? Or what I plan to do if it is still here at 12:01?"

"I know, Chief. It's taking longer than I thought. I haven't found a place to live yet, so I had them bring my stuff today so I can move it upstairs. I don't know if I'll like it up there or not, but it will be a place of my own for now."

"As long as the truck is gone by noon."

"But, Chief, I don't know if that's possible now. I hadn't planned to move my stuff in when we talked yesterday."

"I see two guys going in and coming out. Where are all the extra people you have working here? Why aren't they helping?"

"The girls are upstairs cleaning the living area for me. I don't think anyone's lived up there in ages and I can't unpack until it's cleaned."

Conrad huffed. "You can all clean house when the rig is gone. Right now, you need everybody you have out here in this street moving these boxes inside because at 12:01 today I will ticket and tow this truck off Fennel Street. Do you understand me?"

"But you can't do that!" Regina advanced again and raised her voice.

Conrad pulled Briscoe close to lean him against his leg. "I can and I will."

Regina stepped back and huffed. "So much for the congenial small-town welcome."

"You had that welcome yesterday despite the fact that you systematically shutdown all of these people's livelihood without a single consideration for them at all. None of these storefronts can get any business because you are blocking the street and all the parking."

Regina looked around the street avoiding Conrad's gaze. "I'm sorry."

"Don't tell me. Tell them. You owe them all an apology and if you aren't going to be considerate enough to move that rig to the community center parking lot and carry your stuff down the sidewalk to your store, I will see that it gets moved myself."

"I'll take care of it, Chief."

Conrad nodded and turned Briscoe around to walk back to the station. They couldn't get down the sidewalk anyway and he had to start working on a plan to move an 18-wheeler. That situation didn't come up often in a small town and it might take at least a phone call or two.

Grab your copy here!

https://readerlinks.com/l/2070073

If this is your first trip to Spicetown and you would like to see more, you can learn all about it in the original Spicetown Mystery Series.

SR

I'd love to hear from you!

Find me on Facebook, or join my email list for upcoming news!

www.SheriRichey.com

Made in United States
Orlando, FL
04 August 2025